JAMIL T. HUIE

GOD
SEX *and*
SLAVERY

THE SLAVE MASTER'S WIFE

GOD, SEX *and* SLAVERY

THE SLAVE MASTER'S WIFE

JAMIL T. HUIE

ISBN:
978-1-7370442–1-5 (Hardcover)
978–1-7370442-0-8 (Paperback)
978-1-7370442-2-2 (E-book)

Any references to historical events, real people, or real places are used
fictitiously. Names, characters, and places are products of the author's
imagination.

Cover design by Tri Widyatmaka
Typesetting and e-book conversion by Victor Marcos

A division of The 4th Registry Inc. family.

CONTENTS

Reality based imagination.

Uncut and raw warning: Explicit language and adult
content

CHAPTER ONE

A tour of the universe

The journey of life has its rewards and burdens and its ups and downs. We all travel through life, but if you look deep enough, you can see the stories of the universe unfold like daises unfurling to the morning's light. The truth never hides. A journey through the cosmos tells many stories. Planets collide, poetic structured chaos. Stars explode and take everything within reach. Atmospheres burn away in an inferno and whatever lifeforms reside, dissipate quickly like they never were. We, the people of the earth, advance at lightspeed in hopes to never meet such a fate. In truth, not all life does.

But and there is always a "but". When we look closer, I mean closer, microscopically closer, you can observe amid chaos new art, new beauty from art expressing the wonders of the universe. Throughout the history of our galactic world, beautiful endings have brought forth even more beautiful beginnings. The universe becomes even more systematically efficient with time and destruction to its construction. We have witnessed lifeforms evolve into something out of science fiction with its brilliance and intelligence as well as grace and beauty.

Yes, the universe is getting smarter. Our stars more efficient, our planets learning the art of sustaining life even better. The more we observe our worlds, our understanding becomes deeper. There are many forms of consciousness in this universe as well as intelligence. And our human race is learning that very quickly. Even on our own planet, the animals' and plants' genius is astounding. Our planet Earth has found ways to sustain us, as our destructive behavior worsens. Our association of intelligence and consciousness to the brain has widened its margins, as our studies have shown otherwise. A brain is not the only requirement for intelligence or consciousness.

As we travel out to the far reaches of the universe, our discoveries become more and more amazing. Our way of thinking adjusts as the universe unfolds its true beauty. For example, somewhere in our universe, there is a sun smaller than ours, less bright, and burns fuel more efficiently that will outlast the universe. A point of reference; imagine lifeforms having a few more billion years to develop in such a solar system. The evolution could be astronomical. How far along are their technological advances? What are their physical traits? What is their level of spirituality? Have they flourished as a species or destroyed their world completely? Even upon destruction, their energy source will remain. So many questions that will be answered eventually.

There are planets with newly formed life that are still learning development, the process of evolution at its finest. Worlds with life that we share a timeline together. Some more advance, and some less advance. Every possible scenario of life is out there awaiting our observation. Our travels through the universe will one day show us the unthinkable. But until that day arrives, our story begins here on earth. Somewhere familiar, at a time not too far to not   remember.

CHAPTER TWO

Formal introduction

*I*t is 1719 in Tuskegee, Alabama, the last week of November, on a beautiful farm. Everyone is outside awaiting the arrival of Johnathan Clay. For today is a good day, as it is every year, the arrival of new slaves to the plantation. It is a joyous moment for all, but a dark cloud looms over this joy. Even though the slaves are jubilant to meet all the new faces, there is another side to every silver dollar. Some of them will not make it through the cold winter weather. The slave masters always stock up on slaves around this time of year to level out their loss of profit, throughout the cold winter. Some of the slaves are too old to last such harsh weather.

A loud shout echoes from the field. "Their coming, their coming," yelled Timothy, Abigail's oldest son who is currently nine years old and lighter than the other slaves. She also has a daughter Diana who is six years old and much darker than her brother. Abigail keeps a close eye on her daughter because she is getting older, and the slave owners are cruel to aging young slave girls. They have a taste for youthful flesh that Abigail knows all too well the dangers that lurk nearby. All the slaves gather around and line-up. The slave master's wife, Elizabeth, and his two kids are present to greet the new arrivals. "Good afternoon, Mr. Clay," says James, his head slave. "These are the new arrivals," John responds, "Say hello children." Both kids blurt out with enjoyment, at the same time, "Hello, hello, everyone, welcome home." The new slaves stand straight with chains all around them. Abigail and one of the slave's eyes meet, he does not have a name at this moment, but he seems to have a place in her heart at first glance. Her previous husband died during the last winter and she has been in tears ever since.

James the head slave, approaches the new arrivals and informs them of their duties. He and Mr. Clay usually give them their names, but some were already named by previous masters. Sometimes, more than often, slaves outlive their owners and are resold for a profit. "Hey master, this one here name is Homer," says James. Homer stood at about "five foot nine", strong, broad shoulders. He has been working in the field his whole life. He was placed back on the market for resale after the murder of his prior masters. Mr. Clay got him on a bargain because he is amongst the older slaves, but a highly intelligent one. He has a method of keeping the fields going even during the harshest winters. When other fields are dried up, his master's field was still thriving with the best crops. No one knows his secrets. His previous master allowed him to keep it to himself, as long as he kept his fields looking and tasting amazing.

Homer's secrets may die with him because unlike his previous masters, others may not be as honorable. Besides, he hates all whites. He feels they are evil with no honor after what they did to his master's plantation because of jealousy and hatred. He is no fool, but he sure pretends to be. A gem amongst his counterparts. A survivor who loves his people with all his heart, and dearly, almost too much. He has a history of being a hero. He saved many a folk in the past, but that story is for another day. Some heroes do not live to see the fruits of their sacrifice. Through his journeys, he has witnessed many things, but this journey will not end well for him.

Next in line was a skinny, tall, young black man that stands at about "six foot two". He is a quiet man; he does as he is told and never asks questions. He does not step out of line for any reason. He has survived so far, and he is not willing to give his life up for anyone. "This one here, master, is Williams," shouts James. "Thank you, master," says Williams. "You better watch it, boy," replies James. "Yes sir," says Williams. Williams learns his first lesson: James is not one to play with, especially when it comes to his master.

"This one here is Chub Chub," James says with a smirk on his face as if to embarrass Chub Chub. Chub Chub likes his new name. He is a chunky, short slave who stands at about "five foot three". "Looks like you been eating a little too much, eh boy," says James. "Yes sir," replies Chub Chub. "This one here is Bishop, master sir." Bishop is a strong man. You could tell by his build that he is a hard worker. He stands at about "five foot seven" with broad shoulders and strong arms. He comes from a plantation of strong slaves. His daddy was strong, his granddaddy was strong, and his momma was strong. His previous owner bred slaves like they do puppies at a puppy mill. He forced the strongest male and female to mate and then sold them for a profit. It did not matter if they were family or not. Bishop comes from a combination of two different tribes. He has a very complex and diverse background. "Take these men to where they will be sleeping," shouts James to Abigail, as if she would have not heard him otherwise. As Abigail leads Bishop away, their eyes meet, their minds become intertwined, thoughts shared, fantasy replaces oppression, but as quickly as the thoughts came, they floated with the breeze of the day, unreal to this harsh reality.

One by one, she brings everyone to their place of stay, a small four-by-four space until death shows its ugly little face, and a more able body takes its place. Williams was the most excited, out of all to find out he has his own room. A small room but a room of his own. And though Mr. Clay is a cruel man, he always believed each person should have a place of their own. "A man should end a hard day's work with some clarity," He always says. Williams was not like most slave owners, who placed all slaves in one area like they were wild animals.

Finally, Abigail gets to Bishop's place of stay, conveniently in the back. It was the last one built. They had an overstock of slaves last year and some had to double up in rooms. "Well Bishop, this is your room, the most recently made," said Abigail. "Thank you, Ma'am," says Bishop. "Let me show you around, quickly," she says, as though he would have gotten lost in his four-by-four mansion. She rubs against him as she goes by and instantly, Abigail regrets her actions. Something has taken over. She never felt this way, much less to act so sleazily around a man before. But Bishop has this effect on most women in his presence. They want him instantly, the moment he speaks.

She walks in further to show him around. But there is not much space to maneuver in a small room of four walls. He turns, walks behind her, then notices how sexy and curvy her body is from this angle. He suddenly feels a nudge in his pants, uncontrolled and unintentional. It is one of those damn moments. She turns around, he is already close enough for their eyes to meet, and her breath enters his nostrils. He can smell the sensual scent from her skin. They do not utter a word. Without a second's notice, lips meet with a passion of familiarity. Souls that have danced through the cosmos, once before, bathing in lakes of never-ending love, temporarily separated by an exploding beacon of light to once align again.

Bishop starts to undress her but takes deep breaths to control the motions of his hands. He does not want to tear her clothing. She stops him. "There is no time, Bishop." Her lips find the strength to utter, a disrespectful gesture to her body's uncontrolled desires. He looks into her eyes and whispers, "There is always time." He lifts her skirt and lays her on her back as he spreads her legs. His eyes pop and light up with excitement. Her pussy, so fat, so juicy, dripping wet. Her fluffiness intrigues him.

He quickly gathers his thoughts to the task at hand, he can wander about the stars later. He pleasures her as he leans down to kiss her pussy lips. He knows how to show his appreciation. She is shocked by his actions, but she does not stop him. Never has she experienced such pleasure from a man's lips.

It has only been about a minute's travel and it seems as if time has passed this reality's exitance already. His mouth is watering so much, that drool takes its path down. He wipes it away quickly with no time to waste before supper gets cold. Bishop wraps his lips around her inner soul. He turns around so his hips align with her head. He gets his hands exactly right to spread her pussy lips open so he can taste every inch of her. He cradles his hands under her thighs and uses his fingers to hold one end of each lip open. You can see the juices glide down her luscious lips. She feels a little uneasy at first, but once Bishop's tongue begins to glide up and down her thighs and pussy, her uneasiness transforms into an uncontrolled pleasure.

Her pussy begins to squeeze and release, begging the universe for more. He slides his tongue down the right side of her lips, it pulsates in pleasure. Bishop is enjoying every second of it, more than she could imagine as he watches her pussy's reaction with everything that he does. He places his index finger and thumb on both sides of her pussy lips. They open to reveal her clitoris. He keeps track of the time in his head while he works her into submission. A talented man can multitask with the best of them. He begins to stroke her clitoris with his tongue, slow enough not to rush her orgasm but fast enough to get a timely explosion. She is already at the peak of her climax. She begins to moan uncontrollably, her legs and arms shaking without command. The faintness of the mind is on the horizon. Her hands hold on to the bed in an attempt to tear it open. She grabs Bishop's shoulder with one hand and the bed with the other. Breathing is excessive and rapid.

She has had enough as her pussy is begging him to stop but Bishop's grip will not allow it. The flow of the ocean is pouring down with vengeance. He continues the motions of his tongue; each stroke comes with long-term experience. Screams begin to come to life, her body shivers, an eruption of unknown origin. Her hands cover her mouth as though the neighbors are in restful sleep. He releases her lips. Abigail thinks her journey is ended but Bishop places two fingers inside her slowly, her body is now shaking, her mind floats to a faraway land, giving her continuous orgasms, each one more intense than the last. She is overly pleased; the gates of heaven await her. As he rests his fingers in her orgasmic entrance, her beliefs have now shifted. She never imagined a woman could climax so hard and so often, in such a short time. The way she gazes at Bishop comes with a cost of high frequent heart palpitations. As he gently removes his upper extremities and magic wand from her insides, her reaction is one of shock and pleasure.

Bishop looks in her gazing pupils with the same level of intensity. He takes his dripping fingers and places them between their lips, and both simultaneously lick it dry of all the juices present. They lick it dry with lustful intent like water never once was. Abigail has never had the pleasure of tasting herself before but this man, that was carved by the hands of God himself has brought something out of her that she never knew existed. Once his fingers are cleaned up dry, Bishop turns her around, so her ass was aerodynamic upwards, and begins to lick up all her juices from her pubis to her ass, like a wild beast that has not had a meal in months. Still pulsating from its previous journey, the pussy now ready for another explosion from his actions alone. Abigail's mind is turned out, never to return to its previous location. But his actions were not meant for a climatic pursuit, he was just being a gentleman that cleans up after his mess. A gesture she does not mind at all. She allows him to finish wiping her down with his tongue before she begins to get herself back to respectability.

Bishop pulls her dress back down and kisses her on her cheeks and then her forehead. Abigail walks out of the room and enters a new dimension. She walks with giggling paranoia, as though everyone knew what just occurred. Joy occupies her heart and face. Undigested butterflies play catch and release, as they fly freely in a beautiful garden. Her mind unsteady as her feet wonders back to the fields, wondering if the glimpses of the past were a figment of her imagination. But her pussy tells the undeniable truth, as it pulsates and continues to drip rivers of pleasure and satisfaction. It screams for more, she smiles and repeatedly says, "Stop it, stop it, we have work to do," as they both smile with lust and laughter.

"What happen," the startling voice of Elizabeth says. "Nothing ma'am," a quick reply. As she enters the bathroom. She pulls her panties down and squats to urinate and is greeted with a surprise vaginal fart of satisfaction. Abigail paused and burst out with laughter, looks down, and says, "you slut." Her son and daughter yell out, "Mom, are you ok?" She quickly covers her mouth, "Yes I am ok," as she continues her game of amusement and shock tag along.

Meanwhile, back at the room, Bishop lays down in awe of what just occurred. He has no issues with getting a woman, but Abigail, "Wow, what an amazing woman," he says out loud before catching himself. "She is so meaty and juicy, wow." He wipes the drool from the left side of his mouth. "I must have her again." Bishop felt at peace with a touch of amazing. He is enjoying Mr. Clay rule of, first day off. Normally, slave owners would have them go right to work. But Mr. Clay realized working slaves seven days a week, eighteen to twenty-hour shifts was no good for his product. His slaves would die off faster, which means less production out of them than when he has rested slaves. He adopted a six-day, sixteen-hour week schedule. It is more productive, and he gets a lot more out of his slaves than his colleagues. He has twice the production, and he keeps his secrets inhouse, despite the continuous questions of his peers. He likes to keep an upper hand on everyone, which is how he keeps his control.

CHAPTER THREE

Familiar face's

*H*istory and past tendencies have a way of showing their ugly little heads whenever an opportunity arises. No matter how low or diminished value it may bring, an opportunity to shine is well, an opportunity to shine. The Clay family is a beautiful, caring, loving, and loyal example of what a family means on this very land. They should write books and give seminars on how a family should operate their business of life and blood. No one in, no one out. Happiness fills the aura of space, joy that has been but buried under the situations of life. Forgotten but not lost on what once was but still is. But is it really? When one soul does not share the same, it is but a dream of hope that is imaginable.

Quick feet of happiness fill the steps in a hurried motion to kiss and greet the one with the shared circle of eternal love that binds their finger forever lasting, but not their souls or not one soul but the other. The truth may be harsh, but the truth shall remain. Lies are kept secretly true to keep the disguise of power. But weakness shines brightest in darkness as Elizabeth's arrival with hasty breaths to the crown of her royal stay. A sloppy sound of wet skin fills the air. Her hearing enhances to the direction of "hmmm," and water and flesh touching and releasing in a sequence that is not recognizable, but familiar. She hears a woman and man moan. Her mind begins to wonder about the events, putting pieces of pictures together of what it might be before her vision takes the reality of the dramatizing event. Feet begin to flow to not make a sound. An investigation requires silence as to not startle the ones being investigated. Her eyes begin to focus on their pray. She walks into her room to only find her sister's lips wrapped around her husband's cock, in a steady motion of grip and release. Slimes of spit drip from Halle's lips, oozing downwards, as his knees shake in pleasure. Both eyes pause for only a moment to see the intruder but return to finish what is more important than Elizabeth's emotional breakdown.

Johnathan's moans get only louder and steadier as he grabs his eternal flames, extended bloodline hair by the root to indicate no stoppage going forward, it is close to its arrival. His legs shaking uncontrollably, her moans begin to enhance to increase his mental pleasure. His cock gets wider and longer between her cheeks as he rubs its flesh against them. Her spit drenching, presenting an easy road to slide down. "Yes, yes's" filled the room, as globs of semen filled her mouth. "This is amazing," says Johnathan. Halle looking up into his eyes without blinking swallowed his belongings not letting a drop escape. She holds his external extremity with her left hand, squeezes the bridge between his shaft and head for the remains, and licks it all off, eyes still locked on his. Just a friendly reminder of what she has in store for him.

Elizabeth's shock remains fresh as she turns her back and walks out of the room. She has been hurt in so many ways by her husband and now it has gained new ground when she could not imagine otherwise. His unfaithfulness was reserved only with slave girls, especially Abigail. That is why she cannot stand Timothy around her. It is a reminder of her husband's deed and nature. Now he has graduated his demonic ways. But in his showing of power, he has awakened something more demonic.

It is one thing to sleep with slave girls, most of the slave owners do, something that is kept quiet amongst the communities. But it is an entirely different thing to sleep with her sister. Elizabeth has never felt so low, so disgusted, so hateful ever in her life. She has been nothing but a good wife to this man. Kindhearted, reserved, never spoke back, always run to his beck and call, now this. The slaves love Elizabeth because of how well she treats them. "Halle, what are you doing, sister?" with an ocean of tears in her eyes. Halle gets up with an evil grin on her face, wipes her mouth, and walks right past Elizabeth. Halle wants her husband. She appreciates his cruel history. Then Halle says in a low devilish tone, "What you fail to do when you have a good man, sister." Elizabeth just stands there in shock, frozen as she looks at her husband fix his pants with lustful joy on his face. No remorse, whatsoever present.

He continues to get dressed as if she was not standing before him. Then he says, "What? Why are you here?" Elizabeth replies, "Don't Johnathan." "It is already done," says Johnathan. He loves his kids, but he does not appreciate her. He thinks of her as a doormat, that he can just walk over or step on whenever he wants. He has zero respect for Elizabeth, he has been abusing her for a very long time with no threats of retaliation. Not even an argument, nonetheless. Elizabeth does not have the courage or strength to do anything about it and Mr. Clay is perfectly fine with that. It only means he can do what he wants, when he wants, and how he wants.

He walks out of the room right past his wife and looks at her as if she is beneath the trash on a Sunday morning, a peasant. Her head loses its battle in the war of strength and tears come. It has taken the brief colorful atmosphere away from her. How quickly one's emotion can shift from one extreme to the next. Her heart is shattered, crumbled repeatedly. This time, she has not the strength for heart surgery. The stitches of the best surgeons in the world cannot mend the holes that have taken occupancy. Her mind has lost its way. "Why me! Why me!" fills the room in agony. You could feel the pain as each word escapes her lips from her inner depths. The seventh year of renewal has skipped a few years and traveled forward in time. No longer to return. No one could take the mental beatdown this woman has endured for this long without a breakdown. Elizabeth has stood strong for this family. The strength of this woman. Stories will be told for centuries of her endurance through pain and suffering.

"Why me Lord? I have endured. He has no respect for me, I have been nothing but a faithful, loving, and respectful wife, a mother to his kids. Even after all the ill-treatments, I have loved this man. He has cheated and mistreated me, over and over again. Raping slave girls at a young age and falling in love with a colored woman, had a kid with this woman. She and her child work in this house, our home. And I must see his unfaithfulness every single day. God, why, why, why? And now this, my sister Lord, not her. It is too much to bear, I have endured enough." Elizabeth falls to the ground as she begs for answers. "Why won't you answer me?

Silence now fills the room, waiting for the skies to open with a reply to all her questions, the answers to her unrelenting pain. But nothing happens. The disappointment of nothing. Only you and the four walls know your cries. Amid nothing, something more sinister happens. Her mind snaps, no one will see what has occurred beneath the flesh of the innocent but the innocent. What once was will never be but still is. The body rises before the flicker of the morning light in a state not once known before. Elizabeth wakes with new insight into life's blessings and the comfort of knowing what the future has in store. She prepares breakfast, a feat not known to her hands in many years. She has been served for a long time. She does not even know if she has the skills for such a task, but muscle memory takes charge where second nature laid dormant awaiting its opportunity for a glorious return. The air is filled with fresh goodness and loving touch and sensation. Each soul rises with joy from the aroma of digestible goodness. "Mommy, mommy," filled the kitchen with childish voices of excitement.

"Have a seat my loves, welcome home Johnathan. The kids and I miss you so much, we have been waiting for your return." kisses filled his face with love. Mr. Clay and

Halle look at each other with weary shock and confusion as to what is presented before them. A mystery of undesired outcome. The reverse of intended psychological destruction. The vessel remains unscarred to the unseeing eye. Johnathan remains proud and empowered; his manhood has now been solidified. He can do no wrong, his actions have no consequences because he is the master of this world. He knows his wife; she is weak and his stepping stool. He has the authority to do as he pleases, and she has only the right to obey. But a tick has made its way into the vessel's chemical makeup, and in many cases, a slight shift or added ingredient can change the construct completely. The periodic table follows the laws of the universe and those laws stand the test of time.

Smiles of tender goodness fill each cheek with delicious firecrackers of an explosion to the taste buds. Each cheek glides on the clouds of flavorful delight. But happiness archenemy has plans to ruin the current state of bliss. Such a desperate being that will not allow the slightest glimpse of joy only for a moment, a small one. The man of the house decides to speak of traitorous intent. "I am leaving tomorrow for the slave master's convention and I am taking Halle with me, she wants to see how the event goes, she has never been to one before." Such vile, unappreciated words have the courage to enter this beautifully created atmosphere from the one who has been wronged. Normally, Elizabeth and Johnathan would attend the ceremonies together, a form of vacation for the wedded, rekindled ship. Mental silence takes its place in the vessel, deep breaths of planned outcomes trap the moment. A smile of humility worn as makeup, "ok honey, that is a wonderful idea, she can see how amazing the event is, and have something to talk about once she gets home. How long are you going to be gone for?" "About eight days," says Johnathan. "OK, must be a lot going on this year," she replies. Then Elizabeth walks away. Normally, she and her husband would only stay three days before returning home to the kids.

CHAPTER FOUR

Changing of the Guard

*T*he next morning, Johnathan and Halle mount the harness. The kids and Elizabeth stand outside to send them off. Johnathan kisses the children goodbye, and Elizabeth gives him the biggest hug and smile. She tells the children to head back into the house as she follows behind them. Johnathan signals the horses to get moving. Elizabeth's mind drifts as she reflects on memories while roaming each room in the house. Slow motions of hope come forward as she gazes upon the history of joy once lived. Elizabeth lived a good life according to her mother. Her mother has the belief that you cannot control a man's third extremity but at least marry a good one with some wealth so you and your kids can live a decent life. But Elizabeth would prefer a poor but happy life. She chose security over love and now lives a torturous life of deceit, mental abuse, and daily degrading of her being. This emotionally destructive life has taken its toll, she has nothing left to fight for.

Depression and doubt enter the last room, a sanctuary of relief for her ungodly husband. The first place he resides after each journey to release his tension of travel. He has a worktable, a bathtub, a bed, and a few chairs. Everything he needs in his world, from the world. The first thing he normally does is lay in the bathtub that Elizabeth prepares upon his arrival. No slave is allowed in except Abigail, the mother of her husband's son. They both work in the house and she must endure and see them every single day. Abigail serves as a constant reminder that her husband is in love with a slave girl. And Johnathan loves his son that Abigail has birthed for him. But no slave master could ever make such abomination public. This would ruin his reputation, a lifetime to build but an instant to destroy. Wealth and land would be lost, lives would be separated and taken. Reputation is more important than life itself. Death may come upon the lands before reputation is ruined.

That night, Elizabeth stays in her husband's room and cries until emptiness takes its place inside her body. All are gone from what was once there. Her mind drifts on the horrors her husband bestowed upon her through the years. Thoughts of pain invade her mental privacy without asking for approval to enter. Toss and turn won the night as sleep and wake with terror take on a continuous loop of a repeat without pause. A knock on the wooden entrance enters the ear canal, a familiar voice speaks, "Ma'am are you ok?" Abigail asks. "No, I am not, Abigail!" yells Elizabeth. Even though her husband's love for this woman runs deeper than the oceans across the seas, Elizabeth and Abigail have developed a close and undeniable friendship through the years. Best friends, you can say with a cringe. She understands that Abigail has no choice in the matter. Her husband raped Abigail at a young age, and it has been that way between them ever since. Just like Abigail's mother, her mother tried to protect her as long as her strength allowed. But like most men, they get bored with the same pussy all the time. Always wanting something new even if it is not as good as what they already have.

Abigail's mother did all the degrading, veil sexual acts he asked of her, to keep him away from her daughter but Johnathan's appetite was just too big. Abigail's thoughts of fear upon their first encounter always show its little head. Just a constant reminder of her current situation. That is why she keeps her daughter so close to her. So, her experience is not as terror orchestrated as her and her mother's. "Ma'am, can I come in?" asks Abigail. Her lips are hesitant to respond. "Come in Abigail." A pause ensued, then she speaks." Why must he do this to me? He does not care for me. He loves you and your child." Abigail sits in silence and just listens as Elizabeth bears her pain. Her pain is equal, if not worse with no signs of ever-changing. She has already excepted her faith, unlike Elizabeth. Elizabeth trusts Abigail with all her being but she still has a deep-rooted hatred for her because her husband makes her feel inferior to her. Elizabeth just does not measure up in his eyes. Abigail is a beautiful woman; her body is absolutely amazing and stunning. She has had the privilege to have witnessed her naked godliness, several times. Her vagina is fat and deliciously created and when aroused, she drips of slippery goodness. Her husband loves being inside of Abigail, to the point of obsession. But Elizbeth is a very beautiful woman and has an amazing body as well, of equal value but not valued. Her vagina is meaty and grips a man's cock with purpose.

Johnathan makes Elizabeth feels ugly and non-satisfying. The thoughts continue to rage in her head as she lays in Abigail's lap until the morning sun takes its place in the heavens. Silence traps the air, but the bond of companionship keeps the soul rooted. Sometimes silence is the best medicine for our wounds. A lesson she learned from her mother who carried her in her womb, that laid her head in her lap at nights with tears of horror and lost hope. Hopeless circumstances bring defeat when a fight has no light. Our circumstances show us what is, and our decisions show us who we are. Johnathan Junior and Sarah, Elizabeth's kids get up early. Abigail wakes and leaves Elizabeth to attend to the kids and make breakfast. Word spread through the farm quickly amongst the slaves that morning. Abigail made sure everyone was prepared to make it a joyous day for Elizabeth. Everyone loved her so much, it is unmeasurable. She has always been good to everyone, so it is an easy task for them to make her day as good as possible. "Do not, whatsoever you do, call her Mrs. Clay today!" Abigail warns the other slaves. Abigail made sure everyone understood these instructions. She wanted a day free of ownership with her marriage because the feeling of an imprisoned marriage has collected its dust and is overaged.

Throughout the workday, the slaves sing and dance. James plays catch with Elizabeth's kids. "Catch the ball boy," shouts James with an exaggerated smile and laughter. As she watches her son and daughter play, she jumps for joy when they catch the ball. Delight fills her soul, she has not felt happiness since the day it was stripped from her, which was not too long ago. "Yes, woo, I knew you could do it," Elizabeth screams with a smile that could fill two faces.

James brings out the guitar and starts playing in the field while everyone continues to work. They never had a day like this before. Everyone was filled with joy and ease.

They sang, they smiled, they played. Elizabeth laughed and laughed until cramps took her stomach. It has been years if ever, everyone felt so happy. Elizabeth concludes the workday early. She tells everyone, "Go home, take the rest of the day, enjoy your families and kids for once." This has never happened before. And it does not sit well with James, Mr. Clay's, slave general. But he knows he cannot step out of line with Elizabeth, that would not end well for him. "Thank you, ma'am," fills the air from everyone. James's wife, Claire looks in his direction because she feels the same way. The master has treated him and his wife very well as opposed to the other slaves.

That night, while families laughed, ate, and love, evil laid in darkness with bitterness, mixing a pot of deceit and destruction. It spoke with rage and unhappiness to see happiness. The turmoil of selfishness bubbled and mixed until ready. And now, to wrap it up and serve to the unexpected. Thoughts like this bring heat amongst the evil. Bilateral pulses began to hasten their pace, breath sounds rapidly engaged as anticipation ruled the moment. The thoughts of ruining smiles turn the bodies into an uncontrolled passion.

They kissed passionately. James pulls Claire closely and holds her tight as if it were for the first time. As they make love, she deeply inhales his seductive heat and then exhales her seduction into his soul. This level of attraction has remained the same since they first met. James gets on top of his wife; she opens her legs to guide him inside her. Her pussy is already dripping with juices of readiness. It has been so long since the last time. James's cock has reached its maximum potential and is exceptionally hard. He adores his wife. Claire loves her husband's strong meaty cock; he is well developed. He inserts himself in her anticipated structure of captivity. He strokes her with strong slow strokes, her mind already traveled the heavens and is back on Earth. She orgasms before he even enters her. His strokes intensify as her pussy begins to squirt off fluids all over his balls and cock. His pubic hairs are full of white discharge. His thoughts drift into the world it came from. The strength to hold has left him. He explodes inside Claire, emptying his entire soul. He breathes rapidly as if it is his last. Claire loves when her husband releases inside her. It makes her feel complete and special. Like he loves her to no end. The childbearing stage has left her body but the thought of it sometimes makes an appearance. James holds his wife tight as though she is the only woman on the planet. He looks her deep in her eyes to her soul and tells her, "I love you, Claire, with all my being." And she says it back with the same vision. "I love you, James." He keeps himself inside her as they lay to rest. If it were up to him, he would never take it out for eternity.

CHAPTER FIVE

Souls reunion

*A*bigail puts the kids to sleep after an amazing day.

It was difficult to get them to go to bed. The excitement in their eyes would not allow them to sleep. Hopes of future similarities keep their hearts with smiles of anticipation. Their minds rush and thoughts fly with increased speed. A moment of calm was needed for sleep to take its course. But the joy of the day was more rewarding than a night's rest. Abigail's thoughts of the day are flooded as well but mainly of Bishop's tongue painting her body and pussy with wet brushes. A pussy massage of such does the body well, keeps the mind afloat in many ways. Since their first encounter, her mind has not given her the privilege of rested thoughts. It is on a loop of never-ending repeat, but she does not mind, it kept certain parts of her moist with readiness.

Normally, Abigail would never leave her kids alone, but master Clay is away, and she feels it is safe for her daughter to be alone with her brother for a few minutes. So, she decides to head off to Bishop's room. An unfamiliar sound at such a time is heard by Bishop, Knock, knock. Uncertain at a response to give. Bishop says, "Who is it?" Then a hesitant answer follows, "It's me," Abigail says softly. The door immediately flies opens like something supernatural had moved it. Hands of strength and aggressive desire reach out and grab her. She flies into the air, floating. From here on, all thoughts surrendered to this moment of intense passion.

Kissing deeply attempting to reach the soul, Bishop holds her by the cheeks, looks into her beautiful eyes, and says, "You so beautiful, and your body is amazing." Abigail freezes in time. She has never heard words spoken in such a manner to her beforehand. In turn, she takes over, grabs him by the shirt, and begins kissing him. The world feels like it has just ended at that moment, but the end was not cared for because she has now lived a full life. Her body speaks with actions of pulsating movements, endless love, and sweet juices. Bishop had a room with very little adjustment capabilities but that made it even better for secure positioning. Bishop uses the walls for balancing himself, he did not want to miss any corner of her pussy once they began. It has been long anticipated, and she is finally here, he needs every part of her. He takes her clothes off, then proceeds to remove his own. His movements quick and precise, you would think the sun's flames were trickling down its last seconds of existence.

He lays her on the bed and spreads her legs open, holding them firmly. He notices her ass is dripping wet from what is coming out from inside of her, an everlasting flow of fluids. His mouth suddenly dry realizes that an oasis awaits. Her beauty and sexiness are astounding, an unmatched combination. Her beautiful facial features, the curves of her body, her fat, meaty, deliciously structured pussy. His cock is begging to be inside. He takes a deep breath, and finally, the moment arrives, he inserts his hard blackness inside her, pauses in the moment, breaths of amazement in place, eyes glance with skepticism, thinking of where he has been his whole life. He slowly glides his cock between her lips, his eyes never depart from their origin. She stares back, love has taken control. His hard-strong cock fits her inside perfectly, as though it was made just for her. Her mind unlocks endless possibilities. Her comfort level is uneasy at first from his firm grip of her wide-open legs, but the feeling of him inside her is so amazing that the uneasiness disappears quickly. Her breaths get deeper, Bishop places both his feet on the wall to balance his movements. He needs to feel every inch, every corner of her and he does not want to waste any movements. Bishop fucks like he has been doing it his whole life. His strokes continue, slowly and deeply. Every stroke matter, no wasted movements. The pleasure she feels from each stroke is strong and passionate, he feels as hard as steel. Her soul is snatched from her each time. "How can anything be so good," she thinks to herself. Her breath is wiped away with each stroke.

Bishop's stare continues to bring her over the top. Her pussy is in heaven, as he strokes in and out of her, it splashes with the wetness of approval for this amazing man to continue. His cock glistens with flavor. Abigail grabs his arm, then grabs his waist, then grabs his shoulder, her mind long gone. Explosion sets on a collision course. "Don't stop, Bishop, please don't stop." Her yells get louder, her body loses its way. "Oh Gods," fills the room. She yells, she moves, she grabs, she moans. No control is present. The body and mind drift to the parallels of the universe. Her pussy tightens and loosens, it splashes and gushes out continuously. Splash, splash, splash with each powerful stroke. Her legs shake, moans get louder, "Mmmm, Mmmmmm, Mmmmmmmm," she yells to the extent of her lungs. She tries not to be too loud. Her body shakes with zero control. Bishop pulls out, her pussy reacts with a gush of water all over his bed as she rolls and shakes back and forth. Bishop's desire for her is only enhanced by the current events. Her uncontrollable behavior is extremely sexy. "Oh God, Oh God, Oh God," on repeat, until she finally stops. Her legs shake continuously.

Abigail looks at Bishop, knowing she just is in love for all the wrong reasons. She opens her legs as they are still shaking and tells him, "Come here." She reaches out her hands and grabs his hard, strong blackness, and inserts it inside her once more. She looks him in his eyes, pulls him closer, "That was amazing." Deep breath, her soul escapees her vessel. Bishop feels the chills down his spine, as the words left her lips. He then holds her tightly with love. Passionate stokes pursued the moment. Never has his being felt such deep untamed love for anyone before. The feelings that capture Bishop are intense in its presence, unmeasurable intensity. Control has left the building and gives way to passion and love. With his eyes now rolling in the back of his head, his legs shake with pleasure, his mind a distant journey into the abyss of the universe and arms of steel holding her tightly, he ejaculates his entire self, inside her. His motion and screams are unfamiliar to him. His energy leaves with the sperm. His head timbers to rest on top of her bosom. Abigail wraps her hands around him and hugs him with the intent of transference. All the love she feels for him transfers from her body to his. They lay there a while in silence; descriptive words are not in existence. Just energy, dancing off the souls in blissful harmony. Her eyes gaze into his beautiful structure. He violates her pupils with deep stares in search of her soul because she has captured his.

Abigail gets up, holds his head, and kisses his cheek. "That was wonderful, Bishop." She said with giggles and smiles from the heart. Both knowing she must get back to her kids, she leaves his room, walking in darkness with low flames of guidance as not to be too obvious. But something sinister was lurking, peeking, watching like a thief in the night. Death was in his heart, but fear ruled his decision, his eyes full of tears and anger, nothing he can do, she is the slave master's love, and he would burn the whole farm if she were ever lost. Whatever goodness that was left of James's heart that day was filled with hatred. Because his love for Abigail was beyond this atmosphere as every man that encounters her. She is the forbidden fruit on Mr. Clays plantation. Though she belonged to the master, she never gave him the thought of recognition. James whispers to himself, "This cannot be." Evil has set and filled him and that does not mean well for the rest of the slaves on this land.

CHAPTER SIX

Check

*A*s the sun rises in the morning, the kids are already up playing as usual. Normally, Abigail would have been up hours ago, but someone took all her energy away last night. Her face fills with a smile that seems to not go away, as if permanently painted on her face. The joy of feeling joy, butterflies circling and dancing in her stomach, giggles pervade her heart. Timothy jumps on her bed and Diana right beside him. "Mommy, Mommy," echo the room. Both are speaking at the same time. "Are you going to make breakfast?" "Yes, my loves," Abigail replies with laughter. She has never felt so many joyous tingly feelings in a long time. In fact, even with Diana's dad, she never felt such childish giddiness. This seems unreal, she thinks to herself. This energy the farm is experiencing has never existed before. Smiles fill her face while she cooks breakfast, flashes continuously enter the private spaces of her mind, that she does not mind. Amazing, heart-throbbing flashes. She looks around with suspicion, as though her thoughts are on a projection for the world to see.

Abigail quickly finishes making breakfast and tells the kids not to rush while eating. She then heads off to the main house to make Elizabeth and her kids' breakfast. They normally sleep in late anyways, so she is late, but on time. She always gets in a little earlier because, at times, she would do something a little special for the kids and family. Abigail loves cooking and it shows. Her skills are unbelievable when it comes to her meal preparations. Elizbeth is up early this morning and as she walks into the kitchen, she notices a little pep in Abigail's step. She is filled with new, lighter energy, her aura is vibrating at a high frequency. "Good morning, ma'am," says Abigail. "Breakfast will be done shortly." "Thank you," replies Elizabeth. "And Thank you for yesterday, it has been a long time since I have smiled and felt so happy. Just let everyone know the work still has to be done but that does not mean we cannot have fun while doing it." "Yes ma'am," Abigail replies, with a giant smile on her face.

Timothy arrives and Abigail gives him the message. Timothy runs and tells everyone. One joyous day just turned into two.

As we have all come to know, James is not too happy. Especially now, the forbidden fruit that he has desired from day one now belongs to someone else. And once again, someone gets to enjoy and taste its delicious juiciness and not him. Someone will pay for this treason. The last man that enjoyed this treasure, did not end well for him. He did not make it out alive through the winter. James made sure master Clay took care of that.

8

Meanwhile, at the slave master's convention. Johnathan and Halle are having the time of their lives. Food, liquor, and more than enough women to go around for everyone. Halle did not mind the woman being plenteous. She likes to have a snack from time to time. All the slave owners gather yearly for bragging rights on who has the best crops and who accomplished the most. It is the who has the biggest dick convention. The men drank, the woman drank until they could not drink anymore and then drank some more. They hired multiple bands to play music all night long and all day long, non-stop celebration for days to come. Halle slides her hand down Johnathan's pants under the table, she stares at him like she has not eaten a meal in months. And he looks back at her like she is the only woman in the room. Halle already has her whore picked out, a little something for later, a nightcap if you will. Halle takes a shot of brandy and places her mouth over Cindy the hooker's mouth and lets the liquor flow from her mouth into Cindy's mouth, and she drank it down slowly. Simultaneously, they look Johnathan straight in the eyes. An absolute turn-on. Johnathan never had the privilege of being with two women at the same time before. This could get very interesting.

Normally, Elizabeth is with him and they would have been asleep by now back in their room. But Halle is more fun and exciting to hang out with. Cindy says to Halle, "You think he can handle us?" Halle replies, "More than you could imagine." Halle already had her taste of Johnathan, she knows he is a man who loves to be in control, and from her experiences with him, she is more than willing to give up her independence to accommodate him. He is very gifted in the bedroom. Halle leans over and starts to lick Cindy's neck. She has not been with a woman in a long time and her pussy is screaming for a female's touch. The music stops as though it is a sign from the universe of too much fun. The crowd screams, "Heeeyyyyy," a glass is thrown on stage and explodes on the wall. "Who stop the damn music", someone yells with drunken anger. The next band in nervous haste runs to the stage and starts to play, the crowd goes wild, "Yaaayyyy." All the prostitutes laugh at the same time; they are not surprised by the uproar as this happens weekly. Cindy says "Men," then looks at Johnathan with a grin, "Got to love them."

Halle and Cindy get up and head towards the room. "Your more than welcome to join us," says Halle. "I'll be there soon enough," Jonathan smirks, knowing he has no intentions of joining them. Not that he was afraid of a little fun, he already knows that he can more than please them both. He was the type of man who makes proposals and does not give in to the demands or desires of others. The fact that Halle instigated the three-some, Jonathan would never oblige. Besides, tomorrow is another day, and he will have his way with both women on his own time. But for now, he was simply enjoying the festivities. Elizabeth was never the type to enjoy such madness. She always made them leave early and never allowed him to have too many drinks. "Boring," he said to himself. He feels he would never enjoy much of what this world had to offer with her. Elizabeth is a good wife and a wonderful mother, other than that, she is useless to him. "Oh well," escapes his thoughts and into the atmosphere. Johnathan takes another shot of brandy, slaps a hooker on the ass, leans back, and continues to enjoy his night. The morning meets Johnathan still out, he has never had this much fun before. "Can't wait for round two," he yells at the top of his lungs to the blue skies. He continues to walk towards the room with excitement ready to get some sleep. Preparation for another night of partying.

Johnathan walks into the room, swaying from side to side. He somehow finds his way to the bed and falls right in. Halle and Cindy are asleep in the bed with no clothes on. With a smile on his face, he utters in a drunken voice, "Must have been one heck of a night for these two." He instantly falls asleep, lights out like a baby.

8

Meanwhile, back at the plantation, the energy is high. Abigail oversleeps again at Bishop's place. The way she feels in his arms is amazing, she feels comforted, safe, and so much love generates from his soul into hers. Enough to bring tears to eyes and onto sleeves of clothing. She just did not want to let go, even though it was just for the moment, those moments that use to flow through the day have now transformed into eternity. And when the thoughts of once again being held so passionately intrude her workspace, eternity now becomes shackles of the present. Abigail quickly gets up and runs home to make her kids breakfast, then she leaves for the master's house to make Elizabeth and her kids' breakfast as well.

All in a day's work with a smile so big, it makes a full moon feel inferior. The happiness in her heart is overflowing. Elizabeth walks in unexpectedly. "Who is he?" She asked. "Um, what do you mean ma'am?" "Who is the lucky fella? Don't make me ask again!" Elizabeth says with a smile on her face. Abigail froze with chills up her spine as though the past reincarnated itself for a dramatic return. "Well, you don't have to say. And just to let you know, if you do decide to tell me, I will not say a word. I promise, I give you my word." A projection of the past confronted both of their minds at the same time. Silence stood between them, as reality took hold of all emotions. Diana's father was not so lucky. The results of unforbidden love, the treason of the land. The kids run in as though ordained to break the tension. "Mommy, Mommy, are we going to play catch again today?" Elizabeth picks up her son with a big smile, "of course we will." "I cannot wait to tell dad about how much fun we are having," said Junior. Elizbeth sits him and Sarah down. "Never tell dad ok, we will never have days like this again if he ever finds out." "Yes mommy," they both say at the same time. "Promise me." "We promise mommy." Even though they are young, they hate the way their father treats their mother, especially Junior. He hates his dad as much as Johnathan hates his father. So, his mom's secrets are safe with him as far as the kids are concerned. But James is another story, the slave master's pet.

The day started well. James brings out some instruments. The slaves are singing and dancing while the kids run around and play catch and tag, and every game they can fit into one day. James has his plans set, psychological warfare. Not only to change Elizabeth's mood but also how the rest of these next few days will turn out until the master returns. He starts dancing and laughing out loud. Chub Chub knows something is odd because James is acting strangely. He intuitively knows something was up. Unfamiliar territory, clumsy James loses his balance and falls into some of the slaves who were playing and knocks over some of the instruments. He then utters out of his veil mouth, "Sorry Mrs. Clay." Abigail's face turns immediately; all her efforts just went to waste. Everyone was informed to address her as Elizabeth and not Mrs. Clay. She just wanted a few days of not feeling so defeated, so wronged, so abused and so sad. Elizabeth instantly felt all the mental abuse her husband had put her through by the trigger of a few words. It felt like death took over. Whatever joy and freedom she felt has vanished. The double-edged sword of the tongue has made itself present. Only anger and hatred remained. "GET BACK TO WORK, BRING ALL THE INSTRUMENTS IN THE HOUSE. KIDS GET IN THE HOUSE NOW." "But, mom," they both said with resistance. "WHAT DID YOUR FATHER SAY ABOUT PLAYING WITH SLAVES?"

A strange silence overcomes the plantation. Abigail puts her head down. Chub Chub looks at James with disgust in his eyes, just a few more days of peace and laughter and he steals that away from everyone. Chub

43

Chub developed a hatred towards James that day. He never hated anyone before, especially his own kind, but today that has all changed. James's evil grin of satisfaction was not easy to hide. But some satisfaction come with a cost. He has awakened something far darker with scars as deep as the deepest depths of the ocean in Elizabeth. She has been nothing but a good and quiet soul to everyone. She has endured the harshest treatments and remained humble and good to everyone around her. Her pride may have been scared a thousand times, but her character held on to whatever good was left of it. She tried to be good to her husband and others. It was the right thing to do. But now, all of that have vanished because of a few words. Whatever she was is now dead. A new person has risen. All from a few words. Well not actually a few words, it has been years and years of absolute abuse and others, especially her husband taking complete advantage of her.

The kids go inside with tears in their eyes, Abigail follows right behind them with similar features. Elizabeth stands up with rage and hate and heads towards the door, James tries to follow. Elizabeth stops him right in his tracks. "No field slaves are allowed in this house. You know the rules of this house; darker slaves belong outside." Up until today, James has been the only dark-skin slave besides Abigail to enter the house. James, with a shocked face, says, "Yes ma'am." "I suggest you get to the field and begin working, a lot has to be done. Make sure to

44

double the production of yesterday because it will not be pleasant." James again responded, "Yes ma'am." James walks away with anger and shame towards the fields to get to work like everyone else. But there are bigger things to worry about. This night does not vow well for Elizabeth, mentally it will be the most challenging night of her life.

The day was long and difficult for the kids. Before the incident, they were happily playing with their new friends. They are too young to understand the ways of this world. They were full of tears and no understanding of what had occurred. In their early lives, they have not known happiness as much as they had experienced in the past few days. The slaves can attest to that as well. The slaves have been working an equivalent of three days in a matter of hours, pushing to meet Elizabeth's demands. knowing it is an impossible task. Tiredness took their core and pain occupied their bodies. With his generosity and giving personality, he is only to blame. Self-worshiper and thriving for self-worth. James, the so and so head slave, the one who is to protect his fellow man and woman no matter the cost, has sold out for a little extra scrap and pat on the back from his master's own hands. Take a bow, you are a disgusting creature.

Elizabeth notices it is getting late, the sun is on its way to slumber and so should the slaves. Tomorrow is another day to get her taste of the other side. Only double the work has been done with the time allotted, which leaves an open door to hell, though unfair, the course is already set. Purposely done for self-purpose. The task was definitively impossible. But Elizabeth did not care to care. The tears of the skies flow in like a thief in the night to steal the moment. Thunder roars with a powerful, frightening voice. Elizabeth's mind is now set on vengeance. They will pay for what they did to me. James has damaged the already damaged. Her mind was at an unstable place with no room for anything to penetrates its course. "Why did they have to disobey my one rule," she whispers. As if it was everyone. "Just a few more days of not being Mrs. Clay, that's all I ask for." That meant the world to her. "Stupid unworthy slaves:" as she cried and cried and cried. "Lord, just a few days of not being Mrs. Clay, that's all I asked. Why take this away from me. I never ask for much, just this one moment of peace. Just a few days, just a few days. WHY WON'T YOU ANSWER ME? Please tell me, why? I have been such a good woman to you, to him, to my kids, and everyone. I just wanted a few days of peace, WHY? ANSWER ME, DAMMIT, WHY?" Elizabeth screams to the top of her lungs until her vocals began to pain, the thunder roars, lightning strikes the sky a symbol of transformation. Silence takes the room, nothing, no answers to her questions. No magical message, no interruption.

Elizabeth realizes she is alone. Loneliness and desperation accompany her inner being. Everything has been stripped from her since becoming Mrs. Clay. All she ever was, all she is, and all she could have been, have been robbed away from her. She is weak, her mind and body have given in. Sleep is now her destiny, but once awakened, who she is or was will be long forgotten. Tick tock, tick tock, the time passes, and Elizabeth passes with the time. Birth of the unknown shall soon arise. And it will not be pleasant for anyone in her path. She will have her day and will never be robbed again. Good luck to all that is around her. Your days shall not be yours again.

CHAPTER SEVEN

Freedom rein

The convention is going well for Johnathan, he is having the time of his life. Staying out late, drinking himself under the table. "The best few days I ever had," he tells himself. No wife to limit his fun, no father to talk down to him, and no kids on his subconscious. Freedom is a possibility. And it came from the blood of his wife. Elizbeth's sister, Halle, is the cause of his new-found love of life. His thoughts ponder. The joy of not giving a care in the world. Drinking and singing all night amongst his peers, who all think they have it all figured out. Halle's flower is dripping with screams of wanting Johnathan's shaft inside it. She has not had any of him since they arrived, which is killing her mood. Her pussy wants to be fucked and fucked very well. It has just been drinking and partying with him most of the time. She has only had the pleasure of sleeping with Cindy and that has reached its peak. She desires something more manly to quench her thirst. Halle has always had a big appetite for her men, but she has an even bigger appetite for control.

The whole night, Halle is playing her cards right, making sure he does not drink too much. She is adding water to his drinks, most men do not know the difference after about three or four. Like clockwork, he finishes his drink, she goes and gets him another. As they sit at the table, Halle rubs between his legs as casual as she can to get a feel of his manhood. Johnathan instantly begins to stand at attention slowly. She stops herself after giving him a slight preview, just so he does not get too hard that he is uncomfortable. She has been around men long enough to know when they are primed and ready for insertion.

The convention continues its course of a wild party as it always does. People are singing, yelling, and throwing glass. Lots of money being spent and made from people just wanting to enjoy the good things life has to offer. Halle sees Cindy from the corner of her eye and runs with excitement to get her and brings her to their table before someone else can get their hands on her. Cindy sits between Halle and Johnathan. Halle then looks at Johnathan with a sharp stare with purpose. She puts her right-hand middle finger in her mouth and moistens them while still looking deep into his eyes. She glides her hand down in-between Cindy's legs, then spreads her lips with the same hand. She inserts her finger inside her already moist opening. Cindy licks her lips on one side and moans as silently as possible with her mouth closed, as though embarrassed because of the rush of pleasure she is feeling. No one has ever made her feel as Halle does. Halle begins to stroke her finger slowly back and forth. Cindy cannot handle the sensation she is feeling. Johnathan has lost the realization that he is at the convention. Halle realizes she has his complete attention. Then, right before Cindy becomes too climatic, she stops what she is doing. She turns her head towards Cindy, they both begin to stare at each other. Halle pulls her finger out gently and slowly, brings it up between them with her finger glistening from Cindy's juices. Halle wipes it on her tongue and kisses Cindy with a deep untamed passion to let her taste what she had discovered during her journey between her thighs. All the men stop and look over and begin to shout, "HEY", very loudly. The pleasure of seeing two women kiss amazes them every time, although this type of action happens often at the convention. But they had no idea of what has transpired. A very intense moment of pleasure, if she did not have his undivided attention before, she has it now.

Johnathan gets up like the world is on fire. He gives them that look of right now and both women get up with haste. All three of them head upstairs and rent a room. Before they could even step foot inside the room, both Halle and Cindy undress quickly and intensely. Cindy locks her lips with Halle's. She begins to lick on her neck while they walk into the room. She takes her shirt off and begins to nibble on Halle's nipples, slow and then fast. Both women are breathing rapidly and deeply. Johnathan is in heat as he watches them ravage each other with pleasure. Halle feels every lick and touch throughout her body and a tingling sensation down and up her spine. Her pussy is literally gushing out fluids. She is already close to climax, it just would not happen, no matter how much she wanted it. It was teasing her to death. She needed a little more to help her on her way. She wanted a hard-strong cock to fill her insides up. She wants it so bad her body is in flames. She gives Johnathan a look of command to do her bidding. He obliges to her demands without hesitation. Halle loves to be pleased. She loves the sensual touch of a woman and the stronghold of a man even more. But what drives her up the wall and wild is watching, especially two people having amazing sex. Nothing gets her more twined and revved up than watching a man dominate another woman's body, while she plays with herself in enjoyment.

Just the strength of a man and his hold on a woman while he inserts himself inside and out of her drives her crazy.

Johnathan already knows what Halle wants. He grabs Cindy by the waist and picks her up, then puts her against the wall. He places his left hand on her thigh and uses his right hand on her lower back to guide her ass towards him. Then, he takes his hand off her lower back and puts it around her neck with enough strength not to choke her but to let her know who is in charge. He then whispers in her ears, "I own you." As her mind floats across the skies, the only words that exit her mouth are, "Yes, fuck me." Johnathan then says, "Good, I am understood." Cindy says, "Yes master." Once those words left her lips, a sexual euphoria enters the room that everyone instantly feels. Rare energy, everyone is at a sexual peak, simultaneously. The tone is already set for what is to come. Johnathan is a strong man with strong arms and broad shoulders. He has worked the fields his entire life and it shows. He stands "six foot" tall. Her eyes rolled to the back of her head as he presses against her, licking her neck. Her mind has already left this world into another. He pulls his cock out as she rubs her ass against him, begging for her well-deserved treat. He places it against her pussy lips, her body begins to tremble, she never had one this big and strong before from such a powerful man. He inserts in a slow and sexually torturous way. Cindy wants all of it in her now, it has been screaming for years for such a moment.

Johnathan keeps his right hand around her neck as her legs quiver with enjoyment. She takes a deep breath, and her soul escapes her flesh. She feels like a virgin all over again. At this point, Halle is so wet, most of the bed is covered with it. If it were an inexperienced man, he would have thought she peed the bed. Halle moistens her fingers unnecessarily with what is going on down there, it is definitely not needed. She tries playing with herself, but her pussy is so far gone she can barely touch it without screaming. She strokes the beginning of her entrance, then the outside of it. She makes her way up in a straight line to her clitoris then moves her hand in a circular motion. Within seconds, she orgasms harder than she ever has. Normally, once she gets an orgasm she stops, but the peak and excitement of the moment have her hand and fingers on repeat, and she continuously just keeps climaxing as she watches them both in bliss. Even though she cannot take it, she refuses to stop, this is too good to miss. She must enjoy every stroke, every moan, and every scream. She will continue to finish herself off until they finish.

Johnathan and Cindy are on a continuous bliss of pleasure, his cock is getting shinier and shinier as he slides smoothly with each stroke inside and outside of Cindy's never-ending flow of the river. It tightens its grip each time he strokes in and loosens each time he stokes out. She feels him getting fatter and bigger inside her. She already knows what is to come. Normally, it is a quick disappointment, but she has already orgasmed a few times and she is well on her way to do so again. It is speaking loud and clear as it splashes with pleasure. Now, her grip is getting tighter with every stroke inside and outside. A trick she learned a long time ago. She grips his cock with her pussy each time he pulls out and releases when he enters. Johnathan has never felt anything like this before. He was already finished even before she started her sorcery. Now his soul is lost inside the walls of her spell book. His moans begin to get louder and louder with no control. He brings her closer, and says, "YOU OWN ME DAMMIT," with no realization of what just came out of his mouth. Cindy smirks as her magical center screams from her orgasmic experience. Shivers travel throughout her body as her leg shakes. Both are moaning and screaming in synchronized patterns, "Ahh...Uhm...Uh...y-yes...". Cindy moves in odd movements of uncontrolled muscle spasms, then a pause and explosion with a loud shout as she holds on for dear life to his extended being. Johnathan's body shakes, quivers, and pauses and then he explodes inside her, not pulling out. Not caring, he lets go of his full load. He has never felt anything as magical as this before. He now feels free for the first time without a care in the world. Normally, he is very careful after an orgasm, but today was different. His body continues with uncontrolled shaking and shivering. He holds on to Cindy's thighs and waist as though she is the last woman on earth.

Halle looks stunned like she has just seen a ghost. She stops in her tracks from pleasing herself by what is happening between Johnathan and Cindy, frozen in time as drool escapes her mouth. Her mind, body, and soul are drowned in an ocean of ecstasy. She has never from what she remembers, ever stopped in the middle of playing with herself. It just never happens. She is usually too far gone to ever stop. But it felt like she never stopped, her whole being is trembling on this ride of pleasure. It feels like something supernatural is doing the work for her. Halle's daze subsides briefly, enough for her to attempt at touching herself. But she has orgasmed so many times already.

She wets her finger in her mouth unnecessarily. She glides her hand towards her clitoris, but before she even touches it, it denies her access. She screams in pleasure and breathes deeply as her hand spreads out and her fingers spread apart in exodus spasms. But this does not deter her from going for it once more. Her soul needs it like her lungs need air. She goes for a second attempt with the same results. Screams fill the room, "Ah…A-Ah…Hah, s-shit…s-shit…". Her hand takes the same position prior. It opens all the way and her fingers spread out in spasms as she yells and screams in pleasure and desire for her final release. She goes at a third attempt, three times the charm, breathing deeply and rapidly to make it to her center. Her moist finger makes it to its destination, but her body cannot take it whatsoever. Her will has already taken over. She rotates her finger rapidly in circular motions, her body is tense to the point it cannot be moved. Her legs shake, she screams and moans with extreme loudness as the onlookers stare on with excitement and disbelief, as to what will happen next. She was already finished before she even started. She begins to quiver and turns in odd directions as her body attempts to push her hand away but refuses to stop. She can feel this amazing rush coming and she will not stop until it exits her body. Her hand begins to move more rapidly and intensely as her legs spread further apart. Now, the world has lost its existence, the only thing that seems real is this one moment of bliss. Halle continues to scream and moan, then boom, it hits her like a train. She begins rolling back and forth on the bed, "Ah…ah…Ahh…Agh…S-shit…S-shit…S-shit…," she shakes and yells and moans. Her explosion is unreal to her company of onlookers, but it was even more of an unreal feeling for her.

Halle has never had this experience before in her life to the point it scared her. Her soul, her body was far beyond reach. Her moaning becomes less and more silent as time passes. She enjoys every electrical impulse as it surges through her." Ah…ah…ahh…agh…". Her fingers still spread apart in silent spasms. She places her hand over her center to calm it down. Her orgasm has not stopped yet, it is on a continual loop of ecstasy. Her clitoris is beyond sensitive. She fails to even come close to touching it much less to calm it down, her spasmodic hand hovers. Her body continues to tremble and shake with satisfaction.

Johnathan and Cindy continue to hold each other as they watch the amazing sequence of events in front of them. He remains inside her, releasing whatever is left, watching with eyes and mouth wide open. If time had stopped, they would be stuck in an eternal bath of orgasmic pleasure, which would not be a bad place to spend all of eternity. Johnathan pulls out of Cindy, gets up, and walks over to Halle as she calms down but still has some random ticks throughout her body. He looks deeply into her eyes, thanking her for such an amazing time without words. He sits down and kisses her with uncapped passion. He pauses, rubs the sides of her cheeks, then lays down with her. He holds her with an immense amount of love, not wanting to let go. He just felt free. Cindy looks on with tears in her eyes, she gets up and walks over to them, and lays beside Johnathan. She holds him with her eyes closed as he holds Halle. Ecstasy and bliss won the day, but sleep has taken the moment. All are sleeping with an aroma of love. The one and only victor on any occasion.

CHAPTER EIGHT

Open eyes nightmare

*B*ack at the plantation, the rain continues to pour.

Thunderous roar, giant raindrops make the land known of its presence. Heavy rain with the weight of the world on its shoulders. The heavens are speaking, playing a different tune for every ear. Thunder and lightning accompany, driving fear and terror to the heart. Elizabeth's night was not so blissful and loving. She is scared, afraid of life. All in all, she is just having a terrible night. Her own mind has kept her captive for hours and refuses to release its grip. She tosses, she turns, she sits up and stands. She then lays down and rolls over, but the thoughts just kept on with their rampage. The hatred she had for her last name has now taken her emotions to a place of no return. The haunting of Elizabeth's mind is upon her. The bad treatments, blatant disrespect. But she knows one thing, and one thing for sure, they will all learn to respect her by force or by being a witness to force. No more being weak and being walked over by everyone, not even by Johnathan, especially not by him. Her thoughts begin to shift from being tormented to thoughts of rejuvenation and joy. This is not the joy you get from doing something good but joy from mischief. The joy of making someone bend to their knees. The joy of the fear they will all have of her. Her new thoughts bring her happiness, now her mind begins to finally settle, and rest takes its rightful place.

Elizabeth slept like a baby and woke up particularly early that morning, earlier than usual. She makes her way to the kitchen, and low and behold, Abigail is not present to do her servitude of preparing morning breakfast for Elizabeth and her kids. Even though it is not her time to arrive yet, but Abigail normally comes in early to get a jump on the day. Elizabeth already knows why she is not there, but she does not care. She is upset anyways and will use this to her advantage later. She decides to go out for some air just to get a view of her newly found kingdom. She notices the puddles all over her land from the rain, very muddy and very wet. Normally, Mr. Clay would give the slaves off for the morning or a full day depending on the damage and how much water dries up during the day. This is because they cannot get much done in puddles of rain. Besides, sick slaves equal less production and Mr. Clay prides himself on out producing his competition. But Elizabeth's reasoning has left the building, her plans are different and besides, he is not here to make any decisions, she is. Her journey has begun for her reign of terror and a little rain will not delay her any further. Every move she makes is strategic for her own personal outcome. She deliberately did not instruct the slaves to either come in or stay home. She needed an edge, something to bring a feeling of insubordination.

Elizabeth's mind wonders and drifts, "Yes, I'll show them!" she looks to the sky. Her mind is working in ways it has never worked before. She is a very educated woman who thinks in complex ways. The thoughts of mischief arouse her senses to new heights. What is meant to be shall be as it is written in the skies. Abigail's arrival brings a grin to her face. "Good morning Abigail, on time as usual." "Yes, ma'am. Do you need anything before I start preparing the morning meals?" replies Abigail. Elizabeth looks at her with a face that Abigail is unfamiliar with. "Not at this time," then appears to wave her off. Abigail heads to the house and begins her morning task for the long day ahead. Abigail still has butterflies running rampant in her stomach. She and Bishop have been spending so much time together. She has been sleeping at his place most nights, so her mornings are a rush to get started. She usually waits for the kids to fall asleep and then go on her way for her night creeping of love. She has not been getting as much rest as normal, but it does not bother her for it is amazing tiredness. She feels amazing and overcome by genuine love. She can lay in Bishop's arms for two eternities. She feels safe and the love he generates from his body is so overwhelming. Bishop is also head over heels in love with Abigail. He loves her truly with all his being. But for such love comes with a price. Soon enough, it will be the destruction of them both. Life has a way of giving you all you desire and more, and then test you to see if it is something that you genuinely want. Most people will give it up at first resistance. But the ones that align the truth with their innermost being, fight until the very end to hold on. They get rewarded with something more magical because their truth never gives in. Henceforth the saying, "Be careful what you wish for."

Breakfast is over before she knows it. Abigail daydreams throughout the entire process. Oh, the magic of love while her soul surfs the cosmos with a smile. Her body did the work. "Breakfast is ready ma'am," says Abigail. "Thank you, it smells so nice this morning Abigail. Made with love I see!" replied Elizabeth. They both smiled, but Abigail knows exactly what she is implying. That did not matter to her, nothing mattered. Every day with Bishop was a day in heaven. She has been floating around in joy and happiness ever since their first encounter. And it has been nothing short of bliss ever since. Elizabeth sips her tea with a strange grin on her face that is very noticeable. Abigail can feel her eyes staring while she cleans the kitchen. It brings a chill up her spine, but she continues her daily routine. "Eat up kids," says Elizabeth. "Yes, mommy," the kids reply at the same time. Elizabeth has big plans for Abigail. Let us hope she survives what is in store for her. "Thank you, Abigail, that was absolutely delicious, say thank you, kids." "Thank you, Abigail," says Junior. "Thank you, Abigail," says Sarah. Both kids run to Abigail and give her the biggest hug their arms could muster. They are too young to understand the ways of the world, they only know love at this juncture of their lives.

Elizabeth gets up and goes outside. She notices that James is heading in her direction. "Good morning, ma'am," he blurts out. "Not such a good morning, where is everybody, James?" "Well, ma'am, it rained pretty hard last night, and we were waiting for the puddles to dry up some before we started our day." Elizabeth knows that this is the usual course of action, but opportunity knocks, let us not disappoint and do not answer. She understands you do not ask for power, you take it. Elizabeth says in a slithery manner, "nothing worse than a lazy slave. Get everyone to work, RIGHT NOW. Do not waste any more time." James fails at his attempt to explain, "But, ma'am" Elizabeth intercedes quickly. "Are you talking back at me? Know your place." "Yes ma'am." At that moment, James's joy of his previous deceit backfires and it shatters his chest. He realizes he traded a ruthless slave master for an even more ruthless monster. Something he witnessed with his own eyes. Elizabeth has now taken over the plantation, whether they believed it or not. Even when Mr. Clay returns home, the slaves know who a bigger threat to their survival is.

James is furious. He tells all the slaves to get to the fields and get to work. Everyone starts moving quickly. Williams, Homer, Chub Chub, and Bishop move as fast as their legs would permit. You can see Chub Chub stomach rumbling in motion as he runs to the field. James yells out instructions on where everyone should be. "Chub Chub go check on master Elizabeth's garden and then return. Williams, you work here. Homer, this is your spot." James being careful not to make them work in too bad of an area. He kept sending everyone to different areas of the field. A sick slave is no good to his master. He finally arrives at Bishop whom he saves him for last. Darkness takes over his mind once he gets to Bishop. He hates him. Bishop tasted the forbidden fruit of the plantation that he himself was in love with but never got to have his way with her. "Bishop, over here, you will work this area," said James. "But wait," said Bishop. James interjects, "Are you questioning me, slave boy?" "No sir," he replies. He places Bishop in the muddiest, dirtiest, and the wettest area he could find. The other men know what this was about, but no one says anything because no one wanted the retaliation that would follow. Bishop already knows what is to come. He puts on a smile, jumps in, and gets to work immediately. He just starts singing and working, the singing cleared his mind. Not soon after, everyone starts singing together. Elizabeth watched from the house at all the action. She had a lot more in store for the day. Darkness enveloped her heart and mind. Revenge took its place even when it is out of place. She hates everyone, regardless of color or gender. Just hatred and vengeance filled her.

Bishop continues to do his work regardless of the situation, very cheerfully. His production was not affected by the environment or his work condition. Mind over matter. Bishop is a man, who no matter the circumstances found a way to make the best out of everything. He prides himself on the work he puts out, in life, in love, and in family. He learned the art of turning trash into gold a long time ago. James was not happy about the turn of events one bit. So, he figured he would take a stroll to see how everyone's work looked like so far. One by one, he checks each worker. He heads towards Bishop; his movements get stronger and more aggressive. Bishop's back is turned, he is lost in his work and the joy of the moment, singing, and working. James walks towards Bishop with strong aggression and bumps him right in a pile of mud and water. His whole body is full of mud as he turned around and sits up startled. James, with a grin on his face, says, "Watch it, boy!" Everyone looks on with disgust. "You better watch it, if you know what's good for you!" James speaks with a loud intimidating voice. "Sorry, sir didn't know you was there," Bishop replies as he gathers himself together while attempting to get up out of the mess he was just introduced to. He is covered from head to toe with dirt and mud. You could feel the hate and disrespect in James's voice. "Get back to work boy, no time to play around, like some monkey."

Midday is approaching and Elizabeth has not moved a single muscle. The slaves all notice her piercing stare as if she wanted them all dead and gone. They knew if anyone even made a wrong move by accident, something bad would happen. But their cohesion and ethical workflow kept a steady pace. It is a thing of beauty to see how well they all work together, singing all the way through and helping each other as a family to allow the day to go by as smoothly as possible. "Life gives you lemons, make lemonade." Regardless of their circumstances, they all know without a doubt, all they have in this world is each other, and they must take each day as such. That is why they disliked James; he sold his soul for a few extra crumbs for him and his family only. There is no security for his family after he dies, but the little extra means so much to his selfish being, regardless of how spineless it is.

He wants it, even if it means the death to one or two of his own. Elizabeth finally begins to move, and she makes her way towards the field. Everyone watches her every move for each movement she makes has a purpose. Her eyes laser, her shoulders straight and back, her chin up, she walks with a certain authority and pride about her, looking at each slave member as she walks past. She needed something for the next phase in her plans and she already knew what it was a long time ago. No one knows what her agenda is, but fear took over in her approach. Nothing good will come out of this. James approaches her, "Are you ok, ma'am?" "You are not needed," said Elizabeth. "Ok, ma'am. Get back to work men," says James as if anyone else had stopped working but himself. He is becoming useless.

Elizabeth continues her walk of injustice and deceit. As she passes each man, she looks them up and down, searching for something. But her gaze is of disgust and hatred. She could not understand why she had to share the same air with anyone. The world would be a better place if she were the only human that lived in it. She approaches Bishop. Bishop continues his work like he does not notice her walking by. He is the filthiest of everyone. He has mud all over him because of James's indiscretions. Bishop is in silent prayer that she just keeps on walking. Bishop is a man of energy and her energy is not the same as when he first arrived at this place. Her energy feels ill intent.

Elizabeth's footprints stop directly in front of Bishop. He keeps on working. James's smile begins to spread wider and wider on his face because normally when this happens, something awfully bad occurs to the slave or slaves involved. Some slave owners are extremely cruel and use visual pain for mental dominance. To tame their crop, they treat the living vessel as an instrument of torture. "YOU SLAVE" Elizabeth yells. The perfect choice for her intentions. He was filthy from head to toe, not one part of his body did not have some dirt or mud on it.

Abigail notices Elizabeth talking to Bishop. At this moment, her life flashes before her eyes. She was not prepared to lose Bishop so soon, another man. Her husband was beaten to death by Mr. Clay in a jealous rage because of his love for her. He beat him until he stopped breathing. Tied to a tree, James was to blame, and she will never forgive him for taking her lifeline. Prayers flood her mind in a panic blaze for some divine intervention. "Please God, do not take Bishop away from me. He just arrived in my heart; he is a good man. Please, I love him. Please protect him. Don't do this again." Everyone loved Bishop. He treated everyone so kindly and with respect, man, woman, and child. Homer was watching from afar. Homer is a warrior, who has won many battles that he could never speak of. Nothing he has not seen before. No one wanted this to happen, especially to Bishop. "COME WITH ME NOW," says Elizabeth. "Yes ma'am," Bishop replies.

Elizabeth leads the way as they walk towards the master's house. Abigail's heart and soul are in the mourning. "This will not end well; this will not end well," Abigail whispers on repeat in a frantic struggle. Tears fill her eyes, but she knows she must hold back, keep her cool and let this play out. Elizabeth wears her devilish grin well. Bishop walks with his head down, following his master. His mind races to what is to become of him. A silence overcomes the other slaves as they watch and work in horror. Their thoughts ponder on why him and why now? No sound is heard, just quiet prayers fill their mind, except James who is hoping for the worst. He was ready to do anything his master Elizabeth ask of him to do. He is prepared to pull the trigger himself if she asked him to. James's hatred for Bishop runs deep in his veins to his core. Abigail remains in silence, watching each movement with laser-sharp intensity. They appear to be moving in slow motion. They walk up the stairs, Elizabeth as the lead. Bishop's head remains in the downward position trailing his master. Abigail's breath now seems to have stopped for the love of her life may not be amongst the living very shortly. And anything she does may jeopardize everyone. "Is it ready yet?" asks Elizabeth. "Yes ma'am," says Abigail. They walk inside the house with Abigail right behind them. "Clean the floors," Elizabeth says to

Abigail. Bishop full of mud all over him, each step he takes gets plastered on the floor. "Yes ma'am," she walks behind them cleaning and wondering panickily. Wiping and looking at the back of Bishop, in her mind wanting to grab him and just run away.

They finally arrive at Mr. Clay's personal room and walk inside. Once they get in, they walk over to the bathtub that Abigail had previously prepared. "Take your clothes off, slave boy," says Elizabeth. Bishop freezes for a second in confusion. No one is allowed in the master's house, except for the chosen few that has permission to work inside the house. The law of the land is already broken and punishment by death is a big possibility. And now, he is in Mr. Clay's personal room. Bishop already knows his days are numbered. Why would this white woman do this to him, out of all people? He knows his death will be slow and torturous. Abigail's tears have now lost control for she just realizes that Bishop is already erased from the living. "How could Elizabeth do this to Bishop?" she thinks to herself with grief. "Why would she do this? God no, please God, no. I beg of you. Save my man by any means, please." Abigail cries and pleads to the skies for a miracle. Be careful what you wish for because you will get it.

"CLOSE THE DOOR AND GET OUT ABIGAIL!" Elizabeth says with a commanding tone. "And you... slave boy, the next time I give you a command and you do not do it right away, I will kill you myself. Take your clothes off AND GET IN THE BATHTUB NOW." "Yes ma'am," he replies, careful not to look her in her eyes. He complies and takes his clothes off quickly. As he undresses, piles of dirt just fall to the floor. Bishop was filthy, no thanks to James. But in his filthiness was a prize of perfection for Elizabeth. She hated Mr. Clay for all the torturous emotional despair he put her through. Elizabeth knows the one way of letting him know how she feels, is by allowing a slave man in his personal room and make him take a bath in his tub. The same tub he goes in when he first arrives home. Invade his so-called sanctuary. The place where he cleanses his soul. This is a way of freeing her mind of sorts from the shackles she feels when she is amongst him. And a bonus of introducing the new queen to the plantation, a ruthless one that would spare no deceit or torture in her quest for dominance.

She hated Johnathan, hated him deeply and Bishop is her sacrificial lamb. Elizabeth sits right across from Bishop, far enough not to share the same air as him. He was unworthy of her presence. She instructs him on how to wash, section by section of his skin. "Wash your hair..., now wash your arms and shoulders..., wash your chest and then your stomach and your legs, ass, and cock. Now I want you to relax in the bath until I say get out." "Yes, ma'am," he replies. He was compliant with each instruction without hesitation. Bishop already knows death is imminent so he may as well enjoy the last moments peacefully. But if there is any small fraction of hope to come out of this alive, he would take it, no questions asked. He remains silent throughout the whole ordeal.

Silence commanded the room, Elizabeth stayed in deep thought attempting to figure out, how this will all play out. The anger Johnathan will feel once he walks through that door, the death of Bishop, and the agony Abigail will feel from such a tragic end of her love affair. Abigail remains in tears outside the door, her mind is in disarray because she does not know what is happening inside master Clay's personal room. Her heart refuses to leave the pit of her stomach. She attempts to keep herself busy and distracts her mind from her thoughts. But her love is too strong for Bishop, it has taken over her entire being without notice of entry. She has released herself to him without holding back and now he will be stripped from her without either of their approvals. "How can the world be so cruel and unjust?" Her tears keep flowing. "Give you everything you ever wanted, and then take it away." Her mind is made up. It has developed a sense of stubbornness that she is unaware of. She will not lose Bishop without a fight and if she dies trying to save him, then so be it. Their souls will dance in eternity on the waves of the universe. Elizabeth remains in deep thought; she cannot possibly kill Bishop yet. She hates Abigail for taking her husband's heart and Mr. Clay will not be home for a few days. She must wait for his arrival home to let her plans unfold themselves. Her satisfaction level is at its peak. She has taken away his sanctuary, even if he does not know of it yet. Up until this day, no one has ever taken a bath in this tub but the master himself. The satisfaction of stripping away something from him makes her smile. And the bonus of it being a slave, the people he despises most. He may burn the whole room down just to remove the stench of a 'nigger' in his area of solitude. Elizabeth feels a sudden rush of excitement and anxiety for the next phase of her plans.

"Bishop, get out of the tub and dry yourself up quickly." Bishop gets out of the tub as instructed and begins to dry himself up. His mind starts to feel a little relief. He is granted more time to get whatever he needed to get out before his time in this place is taken away. He wants to hold Abigail with all his soul and hug the kids that he has grown to love as his own. His heart, his mind, and soul belong to Abigail. He has never loved a woman the way he loves Abigail and now he gets more time with her. He thanks the heavens as he quickly dries his skin. "Once you finish drying up, put your clothes on and get back to work. I will call you once I need you again. And the next time you hesitate on my command, I will kill you right where you stand." Elizabeth speaks with death in her voice. "Yes, ma'am," replies Bishop. Elizabeth gets out of her seat to witness the fear in Bishop's face. She walks towards him to receive her satisfaction of a man being afraid of her. A mental drug that is intoxicating. The fear of others towards her. The ability to torture another soul without repercussion. As she walks towards Bishop, her mind continues to go over the mischief and deceit ahead. A seed that continues to grow. She allows her plans to recycle in her mind like a loop that is just repeating itself, over and over and over again. Her excitement grows faster and faster, as though she wanted to command time itself. Her footsteps stop right in front of Bishop, as he attempts to move as fast as he possibly can to get dressed. Bishop wanted to remove himself from her presence immediately. He knew staying one second longer than necessary would equate to the trouble that he was not prepared for.

Bishop's mind slows down to notice she was standing right in front of him. He suddenly stops himself from thinking to escape. Any reaction currently is the wrong reaction. The only option is to stop what he is doing until she tells him to proceed. He has dealt with masters like this before, cruel, and soulless. They work maliciously and slow. They enjoy the course of the game, the torture more than the end. The journey to the kill is what excites them. Seeing the puzzled faces of why? The fear, the confusion of another person. Watching others suffer to fill some kind of endless, empty hole in their soul that can never be filled. Bishop stands tall and motionless out of fear. He looked at his master and then put his head down, which gives Elizabeth joy. Finally, she has control. She has power over her world to do as she pleases. Give someone power and you shall see their true character. Bishop is still wet; he was not able to finish drying off. The sun's rays pierce through a window and on him. The light hits the water dripping from Bishop's body and he glows as if by magic. Elizabeth's newfound power has given her a sense of invincibility. She looks at Bishop's chest and notices the light beaming from it. She has not stood in front of a naked man in almost a year. Mr. Clay has not touched her, much less looked in her direction in so long. She forgot how it feels to have a man inside her. Her eyes scrutinize Bishop's body like an investigator analyzing a weapon to solve a crime. She notices his strong black cock, hanging down and wet from his bath. She begins to feel a tingle through her body that takes her by surprise. She has never felt like this for another man before and a slave at that. Her mouth drools on one side. Her hand takes a quick motion of wiping her vulnerability. Her pussy refuses to listen to reason and begins dripping with gooey goodness.

Elizabeth's body is screaming to be fucked. At this point, she has lost all control. Her legs develop a brain and begin moving on their own. She goes down on her knees, her hands reach out on their own with zero control as she grabs Bishop's black shiny goodness. She begins to rub it with both hands. She begins to drool again, and her tongue licks her lips with approval. She has never seen an extremity that looked so delicious in her life. Her lips are now kissing it all over, from the head to the shaft and back to the head again. Then she starts alternating between licking and kissing it, as if it is the last one, she will ever receive again on this planet we call earth. Elizabeth has never put any man in her mouth before. But there is something about Bishop and the way his manhood looks and feels in her hands that she could not help herself. She just must know what it feels like inside her mouth. As she strokes him with both hands, she opens her mouth wide for entry. Bishop is already solid as a rock to his disbelief of what is happening. She slides his black, hard deliciousness between her lips and inside her mouth and begins to suck away. This may be her last meal. Bishop remains in shock, he was not in shock by the actions of Elizabeth, but the fact that his body has lost control and is enjoying it so much. You can hear Elizabeth moaning as she performs on him. She continues to wrap her lips around his dick and suck continuously. She stops and licks his shaft while holding it with both hands and repeatedly kissing it. Her eyes wide open and staring at it like it was newly discovered gold. Elizabeth's center is now speaking and dripping all over the floor, as she moans, "Hmmm…hmmm…hmmm", ahhh…yea," with Bishop in her mouth. Her legs shake with enjoyment. Now, she feels a rush of blood shoot straight to her head. She orgasms, breathing deeply with him still pressed in her mouth and in disbelief of what is happening. Bishop never even touched her once, but she is shaking and moaning, "hmmmm...hmmmm, ahhhhh...hmmm." Her deep breathing continues but she refuses to stop what she is doing. The more she does it, the more it turns her on. She loves how he feels in her mouth.

Bishop remains on cloud nine as Elizabeth sucks him like never before. He has never slept with a white woman before much less had one suck his dick. His legs shake uncontrollably, "mhmmm...mhmmm...," utters out his mouth as he tries his best to hold on. He squeezes his muscles and grinds his teeth to prevent the inevitable. He also did not want to release himself in her mouth out of fear of her reaction. But the way Elizabeth was going, she would surely enjoy it, if he did.

Elizabeth stops right in the middle of her tracks and gets up off her knees. Bishop stands there stunned, and he wants her to keep going. The floor is full of her juice as she rises. She removes her clothes with her eyes locked on Bishop's, without ever letting go of its sexual grip. She wipes her mouth with her forearm, and then pulls both his arms out, directing him to hold his arms like he is doing a curl. He leaves it stationary and low enough to get her pussy where it needs to be without struggling. Bishop is compliant with all her instructions without hesitation even though he does not know what to expect next.

The silence continued its hold on the room, no words, just moaning and absolute sexual bliss, and pleasure.

Elizabeth has an amazing body. Bishop is shocked as to how sexy this white woman is. She completely takes advantage of him and abusing her power, but he does not mind. Elizabeth climbs into his arms. A jolt of guilt suddenly takes its place in his heart and soul, but his body tells a different story as his extremity remains firm and strong and ready to perform its duty. Elizbeth moves her ass closer to his extension grabs it with one hand as she holds on with the other and slowly inserts it inside her, "Oh my God," left her lips in a deep whisper and enters their space. The first entrance always steals the breath. Her body tightens and releases almost simultaneously. Her pussy hugs his cock like a tight wet blanket. She continues to move very slowly for she did not want to miss an inch of such a perfect structure.

Bishop pulls her closer and holds her tightly. She is tight with the right amount of grip. "Why does this feel so amazing?" he thinks to himself. Elizabeth continues to torture him with her slow movements. At this point, neither could handle the blissful pleasure. Her body feels amazing in Bishop's arms. She has never felt such pleasures before. Her body and mind are trapped in an eternal prison of pleasure. Her juices continue to flow, sliding down bishop's shaft and dripping down his balls to the ground, guiding her on where to go next. She has passed her halfway mark of explosion. She is tightening and releasing and getting tighter and tighter on him as they continue this journey that they can never return from.

Elizabeth has zero control of her body, "Oh yes, oh yes. You black strong nigger, PUSH THAT SLAVE DICK INSIDE ME. Give it to me, FUCK ME, FUCK ME, FUCK ME, YOU BLACK SEXY NIGGER." Bishop holds her tight and starts giving her stronger more powerful strokes. In and out, in and out, you can hear her splashing from a mile away. "Yes, yes, oh yes, you incredible nigger." She screams, "ahhhh...yes...mhhhmmm...yes nigger." As the blood races to her head and her orgasm is stronger than ever before. Back-to-back, nonstop. An experience she cannot handle but just too far gone to care. It feels too amazing.

Abigail is at the door listening to what is going on. Her heart falls out of her chest. She is happy he is still alive but heartbroken from what she continues to hear from behind the closed door. She never thought something like this would happen. She would rather have died and left Bishop on this planet before hearing him inside another woman.

Bishop is getting wider and harder; you can hear him moan. "Mhmmm...YES...YES MASTER...OH...YES, MASTER," he shouts. Elizabeth is like a river with a never-ending flow. Juices continue to cover the floor as he exits and reenters her in a continuous motion. Elizabeth is staring at Bishop and feels like she is in love for the first time as she gets her brains fucked out by this amazing strong Black man. Her entire vessel is in love for certain. She feels him getting extremely harder inside her. She already knows what that means. "Put me down, Bishop," she says. Bishop complied immediately.

Elizabeth drops straight to her knees, wraps her lips around his head, and places both hands on his shaft, one in front of the other. It is already wet from her juices. She starts to rotate her hands while she sucks his cock. She wants to swallow every drop inside of Bishop, and as a bonus, she tastes herself. This is something she has never done before and that is also a major turn-on for her. Bishop was already done from the first motion. She feels him getting bigger in her mouth, which makes her more excited about what she was doing. "YES MASTER...OHHH...YES MASTER," he shouted. Mhhmmm...mhhmm...YES MASTER." He explodes inside her mouth, shaking in every way. Elizbeth is feeling a rush of control again and that is something she absolutely enjoys. Bishop continues to explode in her mouth. She can see the weakness in him. She sucks him with more intensity than before. Bishop screams for her to stop, to the point he falls on the floor with no way of being able to get himself back up. He is completely weak, screaming for dear life and holding his head. "MASTER...OOOOH...MASTER...PLEASE...MASTE R...PLEASE." This made Elizabeth feel even more excited and turned on. The feeling of power over another

79

human being. Bishop could not even push her off even if he wanted to. The fear of repercussion.

Elizabeth keeps her lips wrapped around him and holds it there. She strokes it repeatedly. Bishop continues to scream in enjoyment as this woman refuses to stop. She is sucking his soul out of his body. And then, finally, she decides to stop, not a drip left in him. Tomorrow is another day, and she knows she could have him whenever she pleases. Bishop remains in shock as electrical pulses shoot up and down his body. Blood still rushing to his head as he breathes deeply. Elizabeth's mind, body, and soul go to heaven and back, as she holds Bishop's blackness in her hand. She licks the back of his shaft while staring him in his eyes to let him know she owns him now, and there is nothing he or anyone can do about it.

CHAPTER NINE

Broken

Abigail remains frozen on the floor, face planted on the door as tears rain down her cheeks and soak the wooden barrier. "Why...why...God, why?" she asks, awaiting her answer from the sky itself. Abigail has never been this broken in her life. All that she is, is now lost in pain.

Bishop enjoyed every inch of this white woman's flesh, but he is no fool. This is the ultimate sin; the biggest crime a nigger slave can commit in this white world he resides in. Fucking a white woman, especially a married one, even though this happens very often was forbidden. The white man does not like to feel inferior, especially to a Black man. His past is now his present. Bishop has seen this happen before at his previous plantation with the neighboring plantation. A white woman was sleeping with the Black slaves. Everyone knew what was going on except the husband and they knew once the master found out, the retaliation would be brutal.

8

On this particular day, her husband came home early to surprise her and give everyone the day off. He walks in and catches a young slave between his wife's legs. At that moment, he is in shock. The wife screams rape like it was embedded in her to pass blame. She forced the slave boy to sleep with her in the first place, so technically, she is the one doing the raping. He was a strong, handsome young man and gifted. The slaves paid the ultimate price that day. Every man, woman, and child were hanged, burned, and skinned alive because of this white woman's indiscretions.

As the bodies burned, she still slept like a baby that night with no remorse for what was happening to human life outside her doors. The screams, the cries, and the begging for mercy did not move her one inch. She got away with murder, literally. Whole families suffered because of one woman's lust and unfaithfulness to keep her panties to one man. This will happen again, as it has happened before because of the lust that remains in the hearts of these white devils. Her heart and the hearts of many others like her believe that slaves are mere animals and not human beings.

Bishop understands these facts very well. He knows he will have to be incredibly careful and listen to every command Elizabeth tells him and react to them without hesitation. The lives of the plantation slaves depend upon it. Everyone remains in shock and fear of what just occurred, they all heard it. James himself remains in fear, he knows the implementation of what is happening now. Normally, if it is one or two or so slaves that get punished, he does not blink. Now, even his family is in danger of not surviving. If his master ever found out, every single soul that sleeps on this soil will be forgotten, and every slave knows it.

The horror stories that have passed from slave to slave have been nothing short of traumatizing. Hearing the stories alone brings chills down the spines of the strongest and bravest slaves. It is humanly unthinkable what another human can do to another in cold blood. The slaves must now pull together as this is now a joint effort to keep it amongst themselves. No leaks, just survival for everyone for no one knows Elizabeth's true intent or plans.

8

Elizabeth continues to indulge herself with Bishop, licking, sucking, and kissing him all over, as though worshipping a magical structure. She has been bitten by the love bug and wants him all to herself. She has been sharing her husband for a long time and has grown tired of sharing her fleshly belongings. Elizabeth suddenly rises, looks at him like a home-cooked meal. "Get dress and get back to work, nigger", she says. "Yes ma'am," he quickly replies, hurriedly gets dressed, and heads out the door.

His feet travel as quickly as they can and his head turns and his eyes lock in on Abigail as she looks back, sitting on the floor disoriented in a shower of tears. Bishop's heart breaks in a thousand pieces at that moment. The last thing he ever wanted to do was to hurt the love he never knew existed. All he could hope for was Abigail's understanding that he had no control over the situation. They both realize this would be a problem going forward because the masters always get what they want. That is set on repeat.

Bishop and Abigail both are hurt, to say the least of what has just transpired. Abigail knows far too well what this means. After all, she birthed her master's child, and he inserts himself in her whenever and wherever he pleases. Elizabeth can attest to that. He has done it in front of her several times. It was a degrading act and Abigail always felt ashamed after each incident. At first, it was difficult for her to look Elizabeth in her face because she knew Elizabeth felt so low to witness her husband do the unthinkable. A continuous barrage of direct hits to her mental and emotional being. So, she understands Elizabeth's hatred for the world. She has been subjected to the worst kind of treatments that only her fellow slaves could relate to. Elizabeth is now damaged goods even with so many amazing qualities.

Elizabeth walks to the door, looks at Abigail's tearful face, smirks, and then goes back inside the room. She shuts the door behind her. Her plans will now have to change slightly because of what had just transpired, but it would be a satisfactory change, nonetheless. A most magical unexpected turn of events. At least in her eyes. And no one, she means "NO ONE," will take Bishop or her plantation away from her. She has never felt so amazingly giggly in well, ever. Never…never…never has Elizabeth floated on air as her thoughts drift into limitless happiness.

No one has ever fucked her like that before. She has failed to walk the heavens and back, until today. The day of Bishop buried himself inside her with his intensity and passion, his strong body, his wide, long, strong, delicious cock. Elizabeth is now drooling like a wild animal who has not eaten in weeks. Her mind spins while she thinks of multiple scenarios. And the icing on the cake is that Abigail would finally feel the pain she has endured for so many years. Her hatred for Abigail has grown to the point that torture is the only medicine. She has lost all the mental stability she once had.

Elizabeth's plans are now in motion. No more fake smiles with Abigail and pretend girl talk. They were once basically sisters, but the toll of what Johnathan has done has turned her against the world. She now believes that everything that has happened to her is a result of Abigail's doing. "That evil bitch. Abigail will pay for everything she has done to me!" Elizabeth speaks to herself. The adjustments to her plans have been made with no turning back. The first lesson of the day: expect the unexpected and adjust accordingly but never change the main objective. You can change the course to meet your goals but never, I mean never, change the destination.

8

As Bishop walks back to work, his soul leaves his body and travels to an event of the past. He is at this moment having an out-of-body experience, which to him feels like an eternity, but it was occurring presently. He arrives at his previous master's plantation. Bishop can hear the screams and pleads, begging for life, to be spared, at a distance. Children's cries come to a sudden stop. The smell of human flesh burning. The horrors that occurred on this day, just tragic and horrific. The neighboring plantation slaves were experiencing hell on earth.

The slave master's wife was like Jezebel in the Bible. She has slept with every Black male slave on the plantation and every white man who would have her behind her husband's back. No matter the race or culture, her legs seem to have no shame in accepting cock. Her taste buds welcome all flavors, bitter or sweet. All the slaves knew of her actions and knew one day they would pay the repercussions, whether fair or unfair. This was the world they had to live in. But none of them expected it to be of this magnitude. Most of the men on the plantation had a taste of her flesh, unwillingly. Like her own personal wardrobe, she had a slave for each day of the week. Unfortunately for one young slave, her taste for him was obsessive, to the point of unhealthiness.

Bishop's master at the time was best friends with Jezebel's husband. He has told him several times about his wife and that she is no good. But like most men with pride, he refused to listen. One day. he felt a feeling in the pit of his stomach. Normally, he would work all day in the fields with the other slaves but that day, he wanted to go home to his wife and kids. He left early told the slaves to continue working.

As he walked towards his castle, Jezebel, as usual, had forced one of the slave boys to sleep with her. A slave refused her once and that did not end well for him. The slaves have learned to comply with her wishes and whosoever comes on board to the plantation learns the rules very quickly. The boy had just turned 18, but he had no choice in the matter. He still bears a mind of a child. He was a handsome, tall, and strong young man. His development was beyond his years.

Jezebel and the young man were fucking in the master's bedroom. "If you do not do it, I will scream. And you do not want that. It will not end well for you or your people!" she said with an evil grin. He paused and looked at her scared. Then she laid back, looked to the sky, and smiled ear to ear in victory. She spread her legs as wide as she could, "Now get to work boy." He removed his clothing, her eyes popped open in delight. She had been waiting all morning for this. He walked over to her and entered her sinful flesh.

Bishop is now in a trance as if he is there himself. Her words echo in his ears and send chills up his spine. Fear has now taken over. As the slave boy gave powerful strokes of anger in her flesh, her mind was gone. His blackness had taken whatever was left of her soul. Her center was yelling and splashing with fulfillment and pulsating in pleasure. But in life, many blissful acts may go unpunished, and one may end a world.

As the skies open and the gates of heaven are within sight, the second half that connects the ring of eternity enters his sanctuary. It is now soiled with pain, anger, and betrayal. And just as a drop of a dime, her hands rise to push her intruder off her. Tears appeared where there were once orgasmic figures. Words of fear, which were once moans of pleasure. The young man left in shock, his life would be no more, and he knew in an instant. But for the horror to come, he wished not on his worst enemy.

The plantation was at its end. Tears of blood. The Jezebel is preaching forceful entry. "He forced himself on top of me. He was too strong; I did not know what to do. Thank god you came home, honey." The rage that occupied the slave master erupted to levels of the highest volcano. He had never harmed anyone of his slaves to this day. But the anger that overcame him blinded him to his true being.

The slave master grabbed the boy by his hair and dragged him out to the front of the house. Nail his hands to the tree and cut his penis right off. The part of him that was inserted in his wife and soiled her self-claimed innocence. Her pussy had no shame. And now, it was the cause of suffering amongst the innocents that resided on this land. The word traveled very quickly, the other slave masters got the memo and were on their way to pass judgment, swift and fast. These men did not care if the slaves were innocent, they just wanted to show they were in control of who lived or died.

The young man begged and pleaded, even with the gruesome show on display. In agonizing pain, he still managed to have some self-awareness. He was not pleading about his innocence or his own life because he already knew that he was a dead man. With tears of love and concern and a weak, fading voice, he begged, "Please do not hurt anyone else, I beg you. It was me; they do not need to pay for my sins. Master, please I beg of you." But it was already too late. The situation had reached a point where the master himself had zero control of the outcome.

No mercy was spared that day. The massacre had begun. They killed mothers and fathers in cold blood. Not even children were spared from destruction and torture. Some women were raped before their last breath by their executioner to add insult and disgrace to the soon-to-be unliving. The flesh of the human capsule could be smelled for miles, burning, and burning with life still in its veins. As the screams reached their peak and found new heights never heard before, tears accompanied facial despair. Fear erodes any hope of possibilities.

"PLEASE MASTER STOP THIS, it is not right." He continued to beg. The master grabbed him by the throat, looked him in the eye with a soulless stare. as he completed his task of tying the rest of his body to the tree and surrounding him with wood. He pauses for a second and lit him on fire. Screams of plea continued as a final act to save the innocent. "THIS IS WRONG, NOT EVERYONE, NOT EVERYONE. THEY DON'T DESERVE THIS!" his voice fading, "I beg you, master, stop...stop them. Do not let them die like...." His voice faded into nothing, as the smoke-filled his lungs. Rest in peace young prince, you shall feel the pain of this world no more. Rest in peace.

Bishop's soul returns and jumps back to its original host, back inside his body. As he awakens in full stride, he whispers, "Rest in peace Timothy, rest in peace." His name, this soul has a name. The only name that is recalled that day. The names of the dead shall remain as such, nameless. So many have gone without a name, without memory. Too many, the burden is unbearable. Bishop burst into tears as he returns to his daily routine, but now the weight is.... unbearable.

CHAPTER TEN

Different plantation, same ol'shit

*B*ishop gazes at the sky, squinting at the sun. One of the most beautiful and brightest days of the year is filled with one of the darkest feelings. He looks forward as he continues his pursuit. But his vision is particularly strange, as he strolls across the landscape. He sees men, women, and children, walking, working, and playing. But they are not as they seem. They are half flesh, half skull corpses looking back at him. He sees tears falling from their eyes then disappears in visibly open wounds on their faces and reappear on their chins. The fear in their eyes can be felt in his soul. Some are just going about their day as if nothing had occurred. This was their way of coping with what is to come.

Bishop has a newfound power or paranoia. He can see the dead amongst the living. His soul feels empty for the first time in a long time. He knows this feeling of the end is near. News travels fast throughout the plantation of what had occurred in Master Clay's private sanctuary. The feeling across the board is that everyone wanted this day to end quickly to head home to their families and just hug them and let them know that they are loved.

The devil has found her way to this land. And she has no soul, no heart. She is filled with hatefulness and destruction. The workday has ended, and it is consumed by silence and worry. Bishop made it to his room after a long bath. He lays in his bed empty, just staring at the wall in a daze. He wonders and asks himself, "What just happened? Did it really happen?" Everyone just had the same dream; this just cannot be real. He closes his eyes, hoping that when he wakes up, it would all be a terrible dream. His imagination has now taken the lead. He prays with all his might that it is just a dream.

An injection of reality knocks on the door. He opens it, Abigail enters with silence, not one word is spoken. Their eyes meet, knowing each other's thoughts. Bishop lays down and Abigail follows and lays on his chest. Tears run their course. Fear and relief share the same space in both their minds. Fear of death and the unknown. Relief of a familiar smell and touch. "Oh, his arms, Bishops arms, I love to be in them. I always feel safe when he holds me," Abigail thinks to herself. She understands that she loved him immensely. But what she did not realize is that he is a part of her soul and that goes beyond what we humans call love. She can feel him in the depths of her being.

The morning wakes her up in a spiritual state, a supernatural force shakes her shoulder to make sure she does not miss this magical moment. She gets up earlier than she normally does before her departure to head home. Her true self has taken control, and everything that she needs is already in her and has now taken over and began to speak with no consent needed. Bishop remains in a deep sleep, unknowing that Abigail has awakened. They normally get up together, but this is not one of those days. Once he feels her movements, he always gets up, every single time, but not today. Abigail holds Bishop's right hand and places her left hand over his heart. "You are my soul, my life, my breath, I give you the most special parts of my being. My love, my passion, my thoughts. My body attaches to yours, our souls come together as one. You are me and I am you. Beyond the burning of the sun. My completion, my everything." She kisses his lips as though to seal eternity, a gift of everlasting. Then she walks out the door to head home to her kids. For this day and every other day going forward will not be known for most.

Bishop's eyes open, but he feels something different this morning. Something with a deeper feeling. Abigail is nowhere in sight, but it feels as though she never left the room. Her presence is strong and undeniable. Perfect in its stance and aura. Perfect in every way. Perfect radiation of sincere, passionate love. He feels her all over the room. Every corner, every breath. All over his being, no matter what part of the room he resides, this amazing feeling of completion is within him. Absolute in its meaning. Pure untainted love. The words, "Thank you," leave his lips to heaven's ears. He found something and something has found him, that neither knew they were searching. But the soul, their souls knew all along of what they were searching for.

An atom plus an atom equal substance. And a substance is a bond of love. The universe wastes nothing from its birth. All substance, all energy from the beginning is the same in number, nothing added, nothing subtracted. Once love is bonded, the memory shall remain no matter the distance or change in form. The universe has been through many chaotic states. But an atom's bond is eternal. And so, shall its search remain with never a flinching doubt of failure. 13 billion years until this merger once again. It was well worth the journey.

Abigail arrived home to her kids before heading to the master's house. She holds them tightly with love and concern. A concern of the unknown. Diana knows something was wrong with momma. "What's wrong mama?" Abigail replies with tears in her eyes. "Nothing, I love you both so much." Diana responds, "We love you too momma." Abigail makes breakfast, feeds the kids, and then heads out to the master's kitchen to start her workday.

Upon arrival, Abigail notices Elizabeth sitting on the veranda, swinging back and forth in her chair. Abigail is surprised. She has not seen Elizabeth this joyous and happy in a long time. She looks refreshed. "Good morning, Abigail." "Good morning, Madam Elizabeth. Beautiful morning, we are having." "Yes, it is." Replies Elizabeth. "Abigail, before you get started with your day, I have some new rules in the house until Mr. Clay returns. Once the kids have been fed and are cleaned up, they will remain outside for most of the day, until I say, Understood?" "Yes, Madam Elizabeth." "Good, glad to see we agree. Oh, joyous joy, today feels so exciting and adventurous. I wonder what the day will bring?" Abigail feels those words in the pit of her stomach once she heard them spoken out of Elizabeth's mouth because she knows damn well what the day would bring. She orchestrates it. The taste of power on the wrong lips never ends well for anyone.

The morning goes on as usual as nothing had occurred the previous day. The kids wake up, "Good morning mom." "Good morning my loves," says Elizabeth. The kids look for Abigail as they always do. Once they see her, smiles and excitement have no control. They run to her with big sincere hugs with love only a child can give. "Abigail, Abigail," they say with excitement. "Good morning, we missed you," with wonder in their little eyes. They stare at her unflinching as though she was not there yesterday. "I miss you both as well, my bundle of joys, every second of the day." She returns their loving hugs with compassion. As Abigail and the kids continue to laugh and chat up a storm, Elizbeth is reminded of the stolen property, her husband, and the kids she gave birth to. She has taken everything. Her husband and her kids love and adore Abigail more than they do her. She wants to put a knife through Abigail's chest slowly and stand over her as she watches the life drift from her body. The only thing stopping her from doing so is the repercussion she would have to face from Mr. Clay. She convinces herself that it would be too easy, Death can be a blessing for a slave. She wants Abigail to suffer instead. And she will have it soon enough. But for now, she puts on a fake smile for the kids.

"Mommy, Mommy, Abigail is here." Elizabeth puts on the best smile she could muster up and continues to drink her tea. The same excitement every morning. How could people love someone so much, so constant every day? It makes Elizabeth feel sick to her stomach and less of a woman. As Abigail prepares the table, an intense force of hateful energy floods her. She can feel Elizabeth's emotions towards her and knows she is in for a run. Elizabeth is coming for her and Bishop in many ways. The amazing Bishop, who is like a superhero to most. Elizabeth is now madly in love with him, her breaths are now one with his and she cannot find purpose without him. His absence is unbearable, her heart feels heavy, a part of her being is missing in this very moment and needs its other half before death takes its place.

She feels it now and she will feel it tomorrow and for eternity. A cycle of obsession that will change the course of everything since the first time their lips met with passion and warmness. Abigail understands completely how Elizabeth feels about her man. It is an irresistible feeling that runs deep. But all in all, she understands. She knows, she feels him going up to her spine, her insides are begging for him. Her hands cannot stop shaking, her mind is already on a loop of foreverness. Her body is already experiencing withdrawals until he touches her again. There is simply no cure once Bishop touches you. What she feels is eternal, whether she wants to or not. An unexplained desire that calls her all day long; it calls for her entire being. Sleep is barely an option; eating is a distraction to her thoughts. The desire to be close once more is haunting and is needed more than breathing.

The torture is unmatched and seems senseless, but you know. You know what you feel inside. It draws you in like a magnet. A magnet's sole purpose is to pull to its desired object and hold on for dear life. It is the same with the heart. Abigail looks at Elizabeth and Elizabeth stares back. Both know exactly what is going on in the other one's head and body and neither is willing to give up Bishop. "The next few days will be something to remember," Elizabeth whispers out loud with a chilling voice.

The kids finished their meals quickly with excitement because normally, Abigail would read to them and play with them for about an hour or so until she begins to clean the house and get through her work schedule. But Elizabeth had James come in early to take them out to play. "Good morning ma'am," says James forcefully. She can hear the terror in his voice, which brought a smile to her face. "Good morning to you, James," she replies. Abigail just glances in his direction and gives him a nod. She dislikes James so much that it turns her stomach. Just the sight of him is upsetting, much less to share the same space. You can add Elizabeth to that list of people now.

"Take the kids outside until you are told to bring them back. Am I understood?" Elizabeth speaks with a commanding voice. "Yes ma'am," James replies quickly. He does not want to give her any reason to get upset. He already learned his lesson. The kids object to the request. "But MOMMMM, we want to be with Abigail," says Sarah. "Chop, chop go on. I do not want to hear another peep out of either one of you." Elizabeth gives them the stare as she speaks. "Ok kids, who is ready to have fun,"

James shouts with laughter. "Meeeee," both say with joy jumping off their little skins as they walk out the door with James.

Abigail is already doing her chores as instructed by Elizabeth. Elizabeth's bath is almost done in master Clay's private room. "Your bath is ready ma'am." "Ok, about time!" Elizabeth speaks as she climbs into the tub. She lays in a relaxed, unworried state as Abigail stands beside her with a sponge and a comb. As Abigail washes her master's back, a terrible thought floats through her mind. She thinks about drowning Elizabeth in the tub. It would be fast and easy. She would not have a chance to protect herself or put up any kind of resistance. But Abigail knows the retaliation would be far more severe. Killing a white woman in these times is like killing the pope himself. No matter how useless or insignificant she is to the world, they would wipe out entire generations.

Abigail continues to keep her cool and does her job at a high level as she always does. She washes her back with the sponge, slowly and gently, section by section with grace and care. She does it to the point where Elizabeth nods off in a daze of sleep. Elizabeth loves when Abigail washes her. It feels like heaven. She feels like a queen would feel in her castle. Abigail has this way of giving with so much love that you can feel it through your soul. Not only with her touch but with all things she does. The way she speaks, the way she cooks, and the way she loves.

Everyone feels her love. It radiates off her being like the sun off a white surface. Elizabeth was once gifted with the same kindness, but her environment stole it from her.

Elizabeth's mind is in a state of peace and tranquility. "It has been a while since you've done this, Abigail, I miss those days." "Yes ma'am, it has been a very long time with everything that has been happening, but things happen for a reason." Those words pierced Elizabeth's spine like a one-way train going the wrong way on its tracks. The last time they had this moment, Elizabeth's heart was ripped right out from her chest. As she recalls, she never forgot the day. It plays like a movie in her head on repeat, a flow of destruction. This was the first time she saw the injustice and cruelty a slave must go through. Her world was always protected from such truth. The things they must stand for and endure on a day-to-day basis. How could any human being remain sane with such treatment and a lack of basic human rights?

8

A flash of light rushes past her eyes. She enters a state of recall. She relives that day as she always does. Mr. Clay walks into the room as Abigail and Elizbeth are in the bliss of laughter and girl talk. Abigail is chatting away making jokes. Elizabeth finds herself trapped in a cage of joy and uncontrolled laughing. The world itself has been let go, as it always were when these two best friends got together.

Elizabeth looks up smiling as she notices Mr. Clay walking towards them, she is smiles, but he is not. Something was wrong because she could not recall ever seeing her husband in this state before.

Mr. Clay is in a euphoric state of drunkenness. Not that it brings justice to his next course of action. He is uncontrollable, he yells profanity and brings fear into a place that once was filled with love and joy. He speaks, "Abigail, Abigail my dear sweet Abigail. You have been on my mind all day. I miss you; I need you and I love you." Abigail freezes and finds enough courage to look at Elizabeth. Both are now frozen in body, spirit as well as words. Mr. Clay makes his way over to the tub in their space of sanctuary. He grabs Abigail by the arm. "Come on let us go. Leave this worthless woman and come with me," he says with a threatening voice.

Abigail remains silent with her head down in fear and shame. She learned a long time ago to just shut up and do as she is told. A hard lesson learned, in a painful way. "Jonny, what is wrong honey? what is wrong with you?" Elizabeth speaks in a desperate fear bearing voice. "SHUT UP, SHUT UP WOMAN. YOUR WORTHLESS, I DO EVERYTHING. ALL YOU DO IS JUST SIT AROUND ALL DAY. You give nothing. You cannot even make my dick hard even if you tried. Let me show you what a real woman looks like." As Johnathan speaks angrily, he grabs

Abigail and rips her clothes off in front of his wife Elizabeth.

The fear in Abigail is now noticeable on her face. Her heart is racing because she already knows what is to come. Elizabeth is in shock and confused as to what is unfolding in front of her. But in the midst of all the terror and chaos, Elizabeth cannot help but say to herself. "What an amazing body Abigail has. She is a goddess." Then the unthinkable happens, which changes Elizabeth forever. Johnathan pulls his pants down in front of his wife while Abigail stands there naked, not putting up any resistance. He pushes her up against the wall and inserts himself inside her. A slight moan echoes the room. "Uh…uh." Elizabeth's heart is disintegrated as she witnesses her husband stroke another woman with such passion that he has never shown her. Abigail remains silent and death takes its place upon Elizabeth. Johnathan ejaculates inside of Abigail. Elizabeth returns to her present mind, feeling alive after experiencing death for so many years a million times over and over again.

History has a way of repeating itself with a slight adjustment that is world changing. Now Elizabeth plans to take what belongs to Abigail as Abigail once took what belonged to her. She has no plans on failing. Bishop fills the missing void that has been present for what has seemed like an eternity. Abigail can now feel the pain she has endured for so long. On top of all the other pain, Abigail has endured. Thoughts of vengeance take a nap as Abigail continues to give heaven through her hands and nurture. As her magic comes to its conclusion, Elizabeth drifts back to earth out of her coma of bliss.

CHAPTER ELEVEN

One heart heals, another is broken.

*E*lizabeth stands up and steps out of the tub to dry herself off. She stares at Abigail with evil intent. "Go and tell Bishop to come here." "Yes ma'am," Abigail quickly responds. Before her departure, Abigail attempts to empty and clean the tub out as she always does. "No, leave the water right where it is. Do what I instruct you to do first." Elizabeth speaks proudly. "Yes ma'am," says Abigail. Abigail walks out of the room with her head down.

Her head remains in the same position as she walks towards her souls' completion. "Good morning Bishop."

Bishop nods, then replies, "Good morning Abigail." Abigail cannot muster the strength to put her head up at this point. "Master, Madam Elizabeth requests your presence." Bishop's heart just caves in his chest. He thought it was a one-time thing. Now the danger for everyone's life has increased too inevitable. "Follow me, Bishop." A silent pause between the two as thoughts of the unthinkable roam their minds. "Yes, Abigail."

Their journey towards the unknown but knowing begins, each step excruciating as they walk towards the house that never seemed so far away in previous ventures. All the slaves are in a state of panic now worried for their families and their lives. There is no silver lining, no good can come from this. Bishop's thoughts of the past resurface again, and he feels chills run down his spine. His face bears the weight of his thoughts. They arrive at the master's house and it feels like it took days to get there. It felt eternal, each step happening like it was in slow motion.

Abigail leads the way and opens the door. "This way Bishop," she acts as the welcoming party. Deliberate intent is deliberate evil, planned and executed well by the intender to the intended. The air is empty and cold as Bishop walks through the door. Abigail stops in her tracks and holds the door open for him. Bishop walks in. A voice is heard from inside. "Close the door as you enter." His eyes wander and scan the room as his footsteps move with cautious shivery. He cannot help but watch in awe at this amazing figure stretching in one side of the room with her back turned. His eyes lock in a trance as his brain abandons his feet, left to roam the earth on their own. Elizabeth stands up and only turns her head towards him. "Take a bath." She continues her onslaught of eloquent motion. Bishop's trance guides him to his permanent destination. He is trapped, yet again, in a blissful obsession of desire.

Bishop's hands begin moving on their own to remove his clothing. He takes a second to catch his breath and notices that the water is used. He looks back up and Elizabeth looks back at him briefly only to assure him that it is an honor to bath in her used water, as she continues her motions with her bodily movements.

Bishop sits in the tub to cause no tension. He knows better than anyone what will happen if he disobeys his master's orders. Bishop begins to wash himself slowly, praying for it to end soon. His mind trails to Abigail and what she must be going through. How much more can his love endure? Not very much more, if you are looking for an answer. She will break soon, very soon.

His eyes do not lose their blissful curiosity as to the perfection within view. Elizabeth's movements are so graceful, precise, and beautiful that they are tangled into one amazing structure. The perfection, the trapping aura of it is unreal. If he had not witnessed it himself, he would be

107

in disbelief that something so amazing could exist in this world, our flesh call home. His eyes never drift from their obsession to the moment. He has never seen this side of Elizabeth, but Abigail knows this side very well. Her skills are unmatched. Her naked body is that of a goddess, but her nakedness took second place to the movements of the gods. This is truly the heavens dancing.

Demi plié

Demi plié

Demi plié

Grande ported bras (right)

Grande ported bras (left)

Chaine chaine left to fifth position (right foot in front)

Tondu deriere (left foot)

Back to fifth

Chaine Chaine right to fifth position (left foot in front)

Back to fifth

Pique turn double pique turning a circle

Sauté right on a diagonal downstage right

Pique arapasque

Chasse tour jete

Glisade deriere

Develop en releve and close to fifth

Tondu right prepare

Double turn to land in a lounge

From the lounge, double inside turn to land in fifth

Glisade esemble changment (right)

Glidsade esemble changment (left)

Pique arabesque glissade jete

(Facing upstage) Tombe padeboure

Glisade jete jete jete

(Run to center stage) Plié

Tourette takes the moment. Bishop's hands develop a mind of their own and begin to applause its approval. His eyes have not lost their obsession for such amazement. His eyes are satisfied with what they are witnessing. Abigail is standing guard as instructed. Elizabeth floats over to the table like an angelic structure of beauty. She spreads her legs, like a front split, puts her head back so it is hanging backward from the table. She looks Bishop right in his soul and directs him to come to her with a wave of her finger.

Bishop rises and gets out of the tub in a trance and walks over to Elizabeth. Soap still engulfs his body and water flow down his strong, well-built structure. With his extremity standing firm and strong, Elizabeth picks her head up and looks him up and down every inch of his features. She cannot help but to saliva from all lips she has available. If she could lick both lips as well, she would do so but only one set was able at the time.

Elizabeth was not into wasting any time. She reaches out as if she were worshipping his cock. She holds it and he shivers. Both hands hold his strong, rock-solid erection, which turned her on even more. He then inserts his masculinity inside her, slowly, inch by inch. He feels like the hardest substance she has ever felt. If she were afraid you could not tell because her soul was already screaming in delight.

With each inch, she shivers even more. As impossible as it may seem Bishop gets harder as he moves inside her. Her eyes never leave him nor do his leave her, burning holes into the wonders of the universe. Bishop felt the heavens running through his veins as Elizabeth continues to guide his strongness to its destination. She never gives way to the temptation to speed up the process. And at that moment, he enters her soul, and she is his as the last inch reaches its end. Elizabeth grabs Bishop by his ass and pulls him closer to ensure full service is given as well as received. She has taken complete control; Bishop is now a prisoner of seduction and good pussy.

Elizabeth is now the guide to her mental demise. She pushes Bishop back. She allows him to exit her screaming, dripping wetness halfway as slowly as she can take it, then pulls him in closer, then repeat again and again. Both hands holding his ass in complete control. Bishop already knows to follow her direction as he does not own himself. With every stroke, her goodness falls deeper and deeper in love with the flesh of this chiseled, amazingly strong Black man. She is on the verge of an explosion, splashing with delight while making watery pleasuring sounds. She never knew making love to a Black man could be so breathtaking.

Bishop was already on his way since the second stroke. It is by will alone that he has lasted this long. Elizabeth remains in a trance. "Hmmm, Bishop, Bishop," leaves her lips in such a seductive way, the walls lose their breath. Orgasm creeping closer and closer for an exit. Bishop egos the notion. "Hmmm, Hmmm," as his strokes get deeper and harder. Their eyes never detach from alignment.

Abigail continues to watch as she stands guard. Her heart breaks inside her chest with every breath taken. But something strange is occurring with her skin as her heart does not match her fleshy desires. Her body is on fire with a burning wanting for her man. She has felt his passion with all their encounters but has never watched him in action. Abigail is not surprisingly impressed but in wonderment of how amazing Bishop is. Each stroke is a work of art that has her pulsating with desire. His intensity as he stares into Elizabeth's eyes. The way he holds her with care but fucks her with earth-shattering passion. Fantasies of just walking over and being a part of this cosmic collision. But as quickly as they appear, is as quickly as they vanish. Her heart is too broken for such human behavior.

Elizabeth pretends well to be in control of the blissful event but both she and Abigail know better. This man, this god of strokes. Bishop was and is always in control. Elizabeth's legs shake, her breath is uncatchable. Her mind light-years away into the abyss of the universe. Her soul has now begun a journey of its own. She appears to be in a game of freeze tag with herself. Her body shakes and stops in an eternal motion of repeat. Elizabeth's screams can now be heard across the plantation, "Yes, yes, yes. Hmmm…hmmm…hmmm." Every stroke so intense and so strong, it is unbearable and unbelievable. Her body disobeys her mind. Her orgasmic explosion comes like an atomic bomb and will not leave like an obsessive ex. Her beliefs are now scattered across the room. Reality and fantasy are mended into one. Her center, normally in a game of catch and release, holds on to his blackness like a pair of vice grips not wanting to let go. If she died with him inside her now, she would have died with all her desires fulfilled. Her body now belongs to him, her mind is on the brink of insanity. Her heart has shattered across the globe only to reassemble itself with only one purpose.

Bishop holds on to Elizabeth tightly. His time has come as thunder comes with rain. He leans over, hugging her as if she is the last woman on Earth. He does not let her go. "Hmmm…hmmm," he tries to catch his breath. Whatever control he thought he had, has left the building. Elizabeth is still breathing hard from her orgasmic experience. And one thing that really gets his blood flowing is watching the beauty of a woman once she reaches her peak. His strokes are now longer and harder as he attempts to hold on with no chance of success. "Elizabeth, Elizabeth, master Elizabeth," walks off his lips as he lets his full load go inside her. He shivers with every inch of his body.

He kisses her deeply and intensely to seal the deal of an amazing moment. Tears pursue Abigail's eyes, which are now filled with sorrow. Her reality comes crashing down with no breaks or sight of relief or escape. Elizabeth's heart is pounding and her eyes full of joy and love. Bishop is still holding on tightly, his emotions now in question. But he must play the chameleon for someone is watching and her heart is more important to him than his own.

For every healing, there is a sickness and for every winner, there is a loser. In life, we learn that losing is never really losing. It is just another lesson learned or experience gained. But try telling that to the person that just got burned. It takes time to see the good in bad things or maybe it is just a story to make bad things seem good.

CHAPTER TWELVE

A slow death

*H*er tears drown the floor she sits on. Her mind is now putting together a way to cope with life in an instant. It felt like a dream that had now turned into reality. Because to pretend as such, is to survive. Otherwise, your demise will be quick and swift. Death of a broken heart is painful and torturous. Abigail does not have the strength to live this one through. As she covers her face, she quietly screams in her hand. The tears continue to find a new home outside her body.

Have you ever felt your soul torn from its vessel? It is like separating a mother from her newborn child. It is death with no end. Imagine dying for a thousand years over and over again. And each time you die, you wake back up to die again in excruciating pain. The pain gets even worse than the previous pain, every time. That is what it is like to be in love with someone and then experience the pain they bring you, repeatedly.

That night, Abigail and Bishop just lay in silence for the first time since they found each other. Not one word was exchanged between the two. Abigail tears run down Bishop's chest all night long until sleep finally takes its place. Some well-needed rest. Bishop feels slight ease when she falls asleep. His tears drench the sheets as he holds the love of his life tightly and lovingly. A man is supposed to protect his love and not destroy her. And slow destruction removes the being that once was unknowing of what will take its place in this vessel.

Abigail's day has been nothing short of painful. She has cried all day, expended so much energy. It is now visible in her face and posture. Sadness is one of the worst sicknesses on this planet for all creatures. If you have seen a sad dog in your lifetime, then you know what I speak of. Bishop continues to hold on to his love for dear life. He looks around his small room for answers that will never come. Words leave his soul and enter their space of function. "I give my soul to thee. My one true love, my completion, my life's breath, I give my soul to thee." Then, as the last words leave his lips, sleep takes its turn.

As his body rests, his soul hovers over Abigail to protect her, to calm her pain. For tomorrow is another day and another day brings life. If there is life, there is hope and this journey is not quite over yet.

The next day starts pretty much the same as any other day. Abigail wakes up, gives Bishop a big hug with warm joy. Their souls dance with laughter and love at the sight of each other as if they did not fall asleep together. Abigail rushes home to make the kids breakfast, then heads over to the master's place to prepare breakfast once more for the morning. She goes through her routine, trying to find some sense of normalcy. James comes and picks up the kids as instructed. Abigail prepares Elizabeth's bath and gives her a sponge bath like she did the previous day. She then goes to retrieve Bishop. She leaves the water in the tub. Bishop takes his clothes off and gets in the tub while Elizabeth stretches in ways he has never seen before. Bishop's eyes lock in on Elizabeth like a hungry child locks in on food at the dinner table. Drool runs down the side of his mouth.

At this point, he knows what is happening. His heart belongs to Abigail, but his flesh is weak for Elizabeth. She is stunning and eloquent. And to have two amazing women is any man's dream. But his heart and soul belong to Abigail and his flesh now belongs to Elizabeth. And it is tearing him to pieces. Elizabeth flows across the room with the beauty of the unknown. After her routine stretch, she walks over to the chair. She places both hands on the chair, bends over with her back to Bishop. She then spread her legs in such a seductive way that Bishop's cock rises out the tub on its own. Elizabeth turns her head and their eyes lock. Their eyes never leave each other. Bishop stands up with soap and water flowing down his body, never losing sight of the incredible display before him.

Bishop walks slowly towards Elizabeth. He remains as hard as a rock, ready to go to work. He arrives behind her in heat. He grabs himself with his right hand and her waist with the other hand. She moans, "hmmm…," before he even puts it inside her. She is already in a climatic state. As much as he wants her, she wants him as well. A dangerous entanglement. Bishop inhales a large deep breath. The craving of her flesh has him in hypnosis. He rubs it against her lips. She feels so soft and moist. Then, he inserts himself inside her. Both take a deep breath of blissful delight. It feels like heaven, as they travel the universe in their fleshy pleasures.

Elizabeth feels her heart drop to her stomach and races back up. She has never felt one so hard and strong before. She is lost in a blissful world with no return. Abigail watches in horror. Her soul cannot take another blow of this. It is killing her spirit and mind and it is now visibly noticeable in her physical state. Her only hope in her head is Mr. Clay's return. He is expected back tomorrow. Abigail's eyes are puffy, and she looks as weak as a wounded fox in a trap. Her poster is down, her tone of voice is soft and sad. Her head is down the tears refuse to cease. And there is no one to help her get through this one. Bishop has conflicted feelings that he must carry to his grave. A secret that shall remain a secret at all cost. Too much has already occurred.

The day went by as slow as it possibly could. No one would have imagined the day would come and this is the journey the universe chose for them. The night arrives and at a higher cost than the previous. Abigail is broken even more. She is at the point of dismantlement and does not know if she can live on anymore. Bishop is trying his best to keep her standing, but her entire vessel is already infected with this sickness of grief. Sleep came with the cost of tears once again. Bishop wakes up and Abigail is not there. Mr. Clay is expected back, and she must prepare for his return.

Upon Mr. Clay's arrival, the air on the plantation is not the same, but his ego does not allow him to investigate. The shift of power is obvious, but he is too misguided to notice the obvious. Mr. Clay's mind remains as such. This is his palace, and no one can tell him otherwise. The new crown bearer wants to stay anonymous for the time being. If you show your hand before time, you may lose everything before you even get it. The slaves and kids line up as usual and give him a greeting fit for a king. But his house is no longer his. Elizabeth will make sure he is aware of that when the time comes.

James stands on the frontline as usual. "Welcome home, master Clay." "Thank you, James," Mr. Clay replies with delight and a smile. "It's good to be home. I miss my beautiful wife. How are you?" he asks as he walks over to her and kisses her quickly on her lips, the usual. He rubs his son on the head and lifts his daughter in a short embrace. They unload his things as he makes his way to his private room for a much-deserved bath. He misses Abigail so much. He cannot bear another moment. Truth be told, he misses her more than his wife and kids. But he noticed something off about his one true love. Her energy was off by miles.

Abigail always has a high, significant, loving, radiating energy about her that just attaches itself to everyone around her. She always in every case brings everyone's spirit up. That is her magical gift. That is why men and women fall in love with her instantly. Kid's love being around her. The elderly wants the best for her. She is a giver first. But the brokenness, the weakness is visible across her body. His beautiful loving Abigail. "Maybe she is sick," he thinks to himself, not realizing she is sick from a broken, wounded heart.

He looks at Elizabeth for answers, but she does not utter a word. "Why are her eyes so buffy? Why does she walk with such weakness and depression? This is not my queen. This is not the woman I left a few days ago." In silence, Elizabeth nods her head as if she did not notice anything different. But she knows what was going on in her husband's head. Johnathan feels broken for his precious Abigail. She is miserable and unstable. The one person he loves for who she is. Her personality is genuine and pure. Elizabeth cannot help but grin at her Husband's puzzled face. If she were not attempting to keep her composure, she would have laughed right out in his stupid-looking face. Elizabeth feels victorious now.

The day passes by as it normally does. The only difference is Johnathan has not looked at or spoken to Abigail. He is spooked by her appearance. He has never seen her like this before, so fragile. Abigail is pretty much ok with not seeing him. She has been his victim for a very long time. Where he sees love, she sees many years of abuse and rape. She sets up the dinner table and serves supper. Her meals are like taking a bite from god's own chef. And it seems to only get better the more she cooks. Abigail is just amazing at all things she does. As usual Abigail serves the family dinner, Elizabeth looks at her then says, "Make sure to prepare my bath later." Abigail is stunted in her tracks. She did not think Elizabeth would proceed with her antics while Johnathan is back home. "Yes ma'am," she replies and continues to do her duties as the night went on. But sometimes the universe gives you an unexpected gift. This might be a chance to make peace with her and state her case for freedom from the spiritual torture she has been putting her through. Mr. Clay finishes

120

his supper and goes straight to his private room, barely saying two words. But everyone is thinking pretty much the same thing. Halle is there but she never speaks. She gets up and heads towards the guest room. No one cares either way.

Mr. Clay remains in a flux of confusion as to what happened to his sweet Abigail. So, he just called it a day. Tomorrow is another. He must catch up on some sleep for now. As Abigail prepares Elizabeth's bath in the other bathroom, she must have rehearsed in her mind a thousand times on what to say to Elizabeth. How does she start the conversation? How and what does she say in-between? And how does she end it? Not wanting to offend or say anything wrong or make her even more upset than what she already is. She makes her bath a little extra special with some rose peddles. She has a small window of opportunity she must seize. Moreover, she overheard Mr. Clay and Halle talking about leaving for another trip in a day or two. She must take advantage of Mr. Clay's presence while he is here.

Elizabeth walks into the bathroom and is welcomed by rose peddles, scented candles, and a beautiful surreal setup. Abigail greets her like royalty. Elizabeth's jaw, if not attached would be on the floor as we speak. "Good evening ma'am." "Hello, Abigail. It smells amazing here," Elizabeth responds with uncontrolled blushing. "Right this way Madam, Elizabeth." As Abigail guides her to the tub, she removes Elizabeth's garments slowly with delicacy to indicate she will not lift a finger. Abigail takes care of everything. Elizabeth sits in the tub. Abigail picks up the sponge and places it inside the tub to soak it first. She then wet her upper body with water. Abigail proceeds to rub Elizabeth back in a circular motion, and it feels like her soul is being massaged.

"How was your day, ma'am?" "My day was not bad at all, Abigail. It went by quicker than expected, you know with that man home." They both smile and giggle with a soft delight of laughter. "Most of the day was the usual. How about yours, Abigail?" Abigail pauses before her response. "It was excellent ma'am; the kids were amazing today. And I finally got to clean up that back room, it looks nice. I hope you take a tour once you have some time." "I definitely will, Abigail." Elizabeth no longer bears the burden of being Naïve. She knows Abigail is up to something, she just does not know what yet.

"Ok, Abigail, what is it? Why the cat and mouse?" Abigail pauses for a moment, takes a deep breath, and just lets it flow. "Ma'am, we use to be best of friends and loved one another so much. I can remember us being in the bathroom every day talking for hours and hours, laughing, and having the time of our lives, just me and you as sisters. Our conversations filled me with hope, joy, and happiness. We used to laugh so much our stomachs would hurt in the process. I love you with all my heart." Abigail's heart fills up with warmth as she speaks those words, a smile that only the truth can bring to her face. "I know master…," Abigail stops herself in her tracks. She silences her thoughts and decides not to talk regarding Mr. Clay. "I love brushing your beautiful hair. And our out-of-control giggling like two grown kids. What happened to us, Madam, Elizabeth?"

"Life happened, Abigail. It is a dark, cruel world and we both are fools. We did not understand how evil of a world we live in. People will do bad things to good people, bad things to bad people, and everyone in-between. Young, old, white, Black, and any other race. This is a treacherous planet." A moment of silence between the two takes place, for the passing of the truth. "But I love you, Abigail. I always have. You are my sister, and I am sorry for all that has happened." Tears of asking for forgiveness and tears of forgiveness have set sail, accompanied by grins of happiness.

Elizabeth stands up then gets out of the tub with soap and water dripping down her body and to the floor. She hugs Abigail with compassion and looks into her eyes. "I love you, my sister Abigail. I want you to take the rest of the night off. Go home, to your man and kids. I will finish up here." Abigail tries to interject, "but ma'am." Elizabeth stops her immediately, "Do not 'but' me." There was a quick pause of approval and gratitude, then giggles took their turn. Abigail hugs Elizabeth tightly, "Thank you,

123

Elizabeth." Ran off with a heart of joy, to a place she once and now calls home again. She tells Bishop everything, breathing heavily with breaks of a child who just ran from the play of excitement of adventure. Bishop goes from holding her hands to giving her hugs in excitement. His heart feels free. "Finally, the plantation is safe again."

After telling Bishop all that happened, she leaves and heads home to see her bundles of joy. She feeds them and tucks them in for bed. As she puts them to sleep, her love for them radiates the room. Once they fall asleep, she goes back to see Bishop. They talk throughout the night. Bishop has not seen the love of his life so happy in a long time. He has not been so hopeful without skepticism in as long as he could remember. They fall asleep, talking with smiles of a better tomorrow. With little strength and much sleep, they muster out some words of love. "Sweet dreams my soul." Bishop repeats the sentiment, "Sweet dreams my soul."

The next morning, Abigail wakes up to Bishop making love to her. They indulge in each other spiritually. Their souls connect with an out-of-body experience, floating above their fleshy bondage. Their spirits dance as their vessels made love. Love has been processed in the past but never on this level. Both souls with an awareness of their departure from the vessels that contain them. But what made this one magical is that both souls are aware of each other's presence to the point of structured connection. This is the point of cosmic everlasting. The beginning has found its beginning. Electrons to atoms of the past have found the meaning to their travels across the infinite. The eternal fortitude of a journey to find oneself. Oneself is found, and the fulfillment of one being is now complete.

As completion comes to completion, both vessels stop in a 'what the fuck' just happened moment. Tears flowing, bodies in chills, bodily hairs standing, and flesh is in hives of the unknown. Both are in the know of what just occurred but do not want to seem crazy. So, no words are spoken, just looks of I know what you are thinking and yes, we just experienced that. Abigail gets dress with a pep in her step. A newfound wow of the world that needs some more exploring. Joy fills her space, radiating with a force of happiness. The sky is not the limit, it is only the beginning. All things are possible as she walks with giggles, contemplating on what to make the kids for breakfast. She arrives home but something is off about her arrival. Normally there are sounds of laughter and play. "Maybe they are still asleep. Good chance to tickle their eyes open." She smiles to herself and rushes to wake them up. She attempts her best to creep through the door. She tries to make a silent entrance, but things keep falling so she burst out laughing at herself.

"Timothy, Diana, mommy is home wake up. Timothy and Diana, get up, it is time for breakfast." Her home remains still in its posture. "TIMOTHY, DIANA QUIT PLAYING, GET UP SO I CAN MAKE YOU

BREAKFAST." Panic rises from the pit of her stomach, to show its face, as crisis sets sail. Blood pumping, feet moving with speed and force. "TIMOTHY, DIANA, MOMMY IS NOT PLAYING ANYMORE, PLEASE COME OUT, SO WE CAN EAT BREAKFAST. PLEASE, KIDS, MOMMY HAS TO GO TO WORK. NO MORE PLAYING COME OUT. Timothy and Diana, come out. Please come out...." Fear erodes what once held joy. Tears change their meaning back to fatigue and weakness. Erect posture is now slouched with depression. Words carry a heavy burden.

Abigail's mind now runs away. It is not unusual for kids to be capture and stolen and then resold, in these times. Continued slavery for someone else with no family or even worst. Horrors are now at the forefront. Panic increases its grip on reality. Elizabeth will not care much less understand. Master Clay will be upset, especially about his son being missing. Even with a slave mother, he still loves his son with everything in him. Abigail ran back to Bishop and woke him up in a panic. Explained everything to him as best she could with tears and fear blurting out words of despair and worry. "Try to calm down as much as you can my love. We will figure this out. They could not have gone too far. Fix yourself up and head to work. I will continue the search." Abigail cannot settle at all. But she trusts and loves Bishop. "Ok, Bishop my love. They are my world and I love them with my all. I trust you will find them."

Abigail gathers herself and quickly leaves for the master's house to begin making breakfast. This is the longest, fastest walk in Abigail's life. The tears of her missing children are pouring with no end. Tears with a prayer for some miracle to happen. She is hoping that the kids are just playing an intense game of hide-and-go-seek. Abigail arrives at the entrance. She stops to put her mind together and takes a long deep breath. "Ok, Abigail. We can do this; it will be perfectly fine," she tries to convince herself. She then places her hand on the doorknob, turns her hand, and opens the door. Abigail walks in to get her morning started as she would any day. Walking towards the living room, she hears laughter and play. The wonder of hallucination ponders the mind. "Why would the kids be up so early?" She hears her son and Clay's kids laughing out loud. Then, she hears Diana playing. Her heart jumps in joy and quickly in fear for her daughter. She sees Diana sitting on Mr. Clay's lap playing. His history does not sprinkle innocent play at that moment. He is a known predator of young girls.

His family's history has imprinted the innocence of a child in him. His father got to her at about the same age as Diana. The fear of that moment has stayed with her, her entire life. It was a mixture of fear and confusion. A child unknowing of the scar placed upon her. Her mother could not protect her, no matter how hard she tried. So, her fear and protection for Diana are beyond understandable. If death shall pass with her protecting her beloved daughter, so be it. Abigail's wants and desires must take a back seat to tact. The tears of relief, love, and happiness must be turned off. The wanting to run, hug, and squeeze put on hold. Composure must take precedence. "Good morning, everyone," leaves her lips with struggle with the attempt of sounding normal to the untrained or unaware ear. Diana, Timothy, Jr., and Sarah all ran to Abigail. They love her so much. Elizabeth hated her for the fact that everyone loved her so blindly with compassion and sincerity.

Whispers of hate carry its treason. "What's so special about her," Elizabeth speaks below her breath. "Mommy, mommy, mommy." All the kids said over each other as they hug Abigail. Diana shouts out playfully, "Mommy, Elizabeth picked us up early this morning to come to play. She said that you said it was ok. We are having so much fun. Come play with us mommy, come play, come play." As she jumps up and down. "Mommy cannot play right now; mommy has to prepare breakfast. Maybe after breakfast, ok." Diana replies saddened, "ok, mommy."

Elizabeth slithers her way across the room into Abigail's ears. "Abigail, I have to speak to you about a new task I need to be done today. Give me a few minutes of your time please." "Yes ma'am," she replies with disgust in her voice and posture. Elizabeth leads the way into another room for privacy. Before Abigail could even get half her foot into the door, Elizabeth wraps her hands around her neck, drags her in the room, and pushes her up against the wall. "The next time you try to take Bishop away from me, I will unleash my husband on your daughter. We both know what kind of predator he can be. He has the taste for young flesh, and your sweet precious Diana is no different than a stranger when it comes to his appetite. I will do whatever it takes to keep Bishop. I will kill you; I will kill my husband and everyone in this house if I have to. Try it one more and you shall see to the full extent of where I am willing to go."

Abigail freezes in shock and fear. "Yes, ma'am." Her approach to Elizabeth has now turned into a mistake. She did not expect it to be taken in this manner. She just wanted peace between them and her relationship to be back to normal. But as the sun, moon, and planets rise in the east and set in the west. Abigail's and Elizabeth's feelings travel the same path. Abigail will burn the house down as well for her love of Bishop. The only difference is the people of this plantation's life would be in jeopardy. If those chains were non-existent, Elizabeth would have been a dead woman the first time she touched Bishop. "And you would have been a dead bitch, a long time ago. As well as your shitty husband," Abigail thinks to herself.

CHAPTER THIRTEEN

No pain, no love

*A*s they leave the room, one behind the other,

Abigail puts on her best face to hide her hatred and anger. The breakfast she made that day was to literally die for. Her joy of seeing her kids gives means to celebrate and Mr. Clay requested a special meal as well. But her special meal was not for him; it was for her kids being in good health and not lost. This is Halle's last meal until she heads back home, and her special escort will be Mr. Clay of course, which is alright with Elizabeth but scary for everyone else. Who would have thought Mr. Clay would be needed to keep the plantation safe from his wife?

Before, everyone would be happy to see him go, but now, they need him to stay.

Johnathan tells Elizabeth he will be taking Halle home and it would be a few days before his return. Elizabeth and everyone at the table know it is only a day's travel back and forth. But this is perfect for Elizabeth because it gives her time to continue her abuse of power. "How was your stay sister?" Elizabeth asks as they eat their breakfast. Halle had a double-take. She did not realize that they were still on speaking terms. Her mouth is full of food, and she almost chokes while trying to respond. "It was spectacular." Coughing pursues and Abigail lets out a little chuckle.

With a wide smile, Elizabeth replies, "I am sure you did; seems to me it was the most fun you ever had here. Unless I am missing something. Well, either way, cannot wait to have you back again sister." Halle still recovering from her whole ordeal. "Yes sister, after the wedding I will pass by again to spend some time with my family." In Elizabeth's head, it is not the family she wants to spend time with, but her husband's dick. That little whore. Abigail's fantasy takes a tour as she watches the disfunction. She wishes Halle would just choke to death on the next bite. In fact, she hopes the entire family chokes to death. As they all complete their meals, Abigail begins to clear the table to wash the dishes and utensils. Johnathan and Halle get up quickly to make sure everything was packed and squared away. The slaves gathered their stuff and packed it away in the horse carriage. Everyone is outside saying their goodbyes and safe journeys. Abigail does not want them to leave because she fears what Elizabeth has up her sleeves next. It seems to go up another level each time she acts.

Elizabeth quickly goes back into the house as her sister and Johnathan set off. Johnathan believes she is upset but it is far more wicked. Her devious plan is to begin its course of despair and pain and she cannot wait. Abigail remains frozen in time as the sacrificial peace road off into the sunset. The day goes by slow, and it is agonizing. It was the same routine and very uneventful. As each task becomes complete and the next ready at the helm, her anxiety increases to the unknown. Her thoughts not resting for even a second.

Elizabeth remains in the master's room for most of the day. And nothing happens. Abigail is antsy. The anticipation is dreadful. Her eyes remain focused at the locked door with thoughts of space travel and the building of weapons of mass destruction. But Elizabeth's weapon of destruction is more mental than physical. But you could not tell Abigail that. Her thoughts have already taken off with no brakes. "What is she up to?" The thought runs across her lips as the veins of wonder run across her forehead. But her legs and hands remain on the task at hand.

The night has come to an end and Abigail still has not solved the puzzle of Elizabeth's deception or maybe she is just being paranoid, and Elizabeth is just resting. Abigail tucks the kids in and tells them, "Good night, see yawl tomorrow," as she finishes her remaining chores before walking out the door. "Good night, Abigail." "Good night, Abigail." The kids say in repetition. Elizabeth makes an appearance and sticks her head out the door. "Good night, Abigail." Abigail replies, "Good night, ma'am," and quickly walks out the door. She heads home to get her kids ready for bed. As Abigail walks home, she cannot help but fantasize about grabbing her kids and Bishop and running away to a better place. It would be a beautiful place of peace filled with love and happiness. Their home would be amazing and beautiful, and no harm would come to anyone in their home. But that is all that it is, a fantasy. There is nowhere to go. Nowhere to run.

They would be lynched before they got anywhere, and their families and friends would pay the ultimate price. Abigail cannot live with something so horrifying on her consciousness even if it is an empty fantasy of hope. As soon as she arrives home, she immediately begins to prep the kids for bed. Timothy interjects, "What is wrong, mom? You're moving so quickly." Abigail paused and noticed her pace as well. "Nothing son. I am sorry." Timothy hugs her and tells her, "I love you with all my heart, mom." With tears flooding his young eyes. Abigail takes in a deep breath so she would not break down. "I love you too, son." Unweighted words can lift mountains off your shoulders. Abigail felt so much lighter with the exchange of words between her and Timothy. With her mind running a million miles per second, it took a moment of shared sincerity to bring her back into the present.

Abigail tucks her beloved ones in bed, kisses them both, and leaves them for a night of peaceful slumber. "Goodnight, I love you both." Diana and Timothy remain silent as Abigail waits for sleep to take over their vessels. Abigail has exhausted herself. She lays down to get some rest. It has been a mental and physical tiresome day. But before she could get some shuteye, a soft knock that barely presents itself is heard but not heard. Abigail ignores it. It happens again, and now more noticeable. "But who could this be so late at night?" she wonders. Her mind races. Just when she thought it was a normal day at the plantation, trouble awaits. "Who is it?" she whispers loud enough that the knocker could hear. "It's me, Bishop," with a concerning, worried voice. On a normal visit, her excitement would be uncontrollable, but her innermost wisdom knew better. This was not a spontaneous, loving visit.

Something is deeply wrong. She can see it in Bishop's eyes. No words are exchanged between the two. She walks out the door and just follows him. She already knows death is certain, but she follows him anyway. She will follow Bishop anywhere on the planet, even if it leads her to her death. Her actions show it. Her love for him is never questioning, never backward, always forward, no matter what may occur. She belongs to him completely and him to her. Their journey continues in its quietness to the Clays' house. Bishop holds Abigail's hand with concern and hurt. They finally arrive and walk inside the door. Abigail engages with no questions asked. They walk over to the master's private room, their final destination. Bishop removes her clothing. Still, no words or questions were asked. Her love is so strong that she is willing to give everything to this man no matter the cost. Her welding eyes are her only garments.

Bishop directs her to the bed, lays her down on her back, and starts tying her hands. First, her left wrist and then her left ankle. He walks over to her right side. Before he could tie her, Abigail lifts her right hand. She holds Bishop on his cheek and looks him in the eyes. She says, "Don't worry, I will always be yours." Bishop looks back with brokenness and continues without a word. He ties her right wrist and then her right ankle. Bishop now realizes the world that he and Abigail created shall no longer be. The walk-in front of the bed felt like a thousand miles. Bishop stops perfectly between Abigail's open legs. He takes his clothes off and stands there naked as Abigail looks on wondering what to expect next. She remains restrained looking directly at him, but Bishop is not looking back. It appears to the unknowing. But he is looking straight through her like she is not even there. This brought pain to Abigail's heart.

Even with all that is happening, her mind cannot resist thinking of how amazing her man's body is. It is like God came down himself and put him together perfectly piece by piece, from head to toe, which he did. Bishop is rising before her eyes. As Abigail licks her lips and looks on with drool sliding down the side of her face, her mind stops quickly enough for her to notice and she licks it off. Her mind is racing, her body is yearning, her heart is exploding, and her pussy has not stopped dripping since he stood in front of her, without even touching her. This man turns her on to that extent and more.

Bishop remains perfectly still with his magnificent structure on display. His blackness remains undisciplined. Something is happening in the background. Elizabeth gracefully walks into the room with no clothes on. Her body is painfully gorgeous. As she slowly and gracefully dances her way to Bishop, each movement is deliberate in its intent. She wants to destroy Abigail slowly and methodically. Abigail's mind goes into a panic. Whatever she felt before quickly dissolves itself. Now, agony took its place, silence filled the room differently for each person. Tears fill Abigail's eyelids as she knows what is to come next with no way of doing anything about it. Elizabeth stops her movements of grace right between

Abigail's legs and in front of Bishop's standing extremity. Her eyes now with a dead stare into Abigail's eyes with fierce purpose. Their eyes lock with focus. Elizabeth bends over slowly with so much sexiness that it moves the clouds in the sky. Eyes never losing their contact. So wet with desire and obsession that it is sliding down her thighs like a flowing river.

Abigail sees her man behind this naked goddess, standing strong and firm. He engages forward towards her nakedness, packaged and ready for delivery. Elizabeth puts her hand behind her, grabs his ass to pull him closer. Abigail's heart is collapsing in real-time. Pain is so excruciating; it feels as though she is having a heart attack. She whispers the pain, only she could hear. "No, not this." You can see the death in Abigail's eyes. She dies with every movement Bishop makes.

Elizabeth is only getting turned on more and more with the pain she inflicts on Abigail. Her center speaks loudly as confirmation. Bishop remains standing firm with his head at the doorway to Elizabeth's soul. Elizabeth's legs are soaking wet from the uncontrollable juices flowing from her insides. Her leg movements are not of her own thoughts. Already captured to the bliss and ecstasy of being penetrated by the veiny hard extremity, that is impatiently awaiting its signal to move forward for entrance. Elizabeth has now warped to a beautiful, deserted island. Bishop now knows it is time. He sends some spit from his mouth perfectly executed, to land on his head. Even though unneeded but necessary for the sexual peak of the moment. It already has juice on it. It mixes as if it were making an elixir. Then he rubs it on the head and down his shaft. Elizabeth trembles with expected excitement. She knows what is coming next.

Bishop holds it with his right hand and grabs Elizabeth's ass with his left hand. He pulls her ass up to expose her dripping door for entrance. He inserts himself slowly with power and ownership. Elizabeth's mouth opens wide and utters, "mhmmm…," as her breath exhales almost in silence to savor the moment. Abigail can see Elizabeth's soul exit her body through her mouth. Their bliss and sexual peaks have found new heights. Bishop places his entire being inside of Elizabeth. She comes multiple times, just from anticipation. Her screams are encapsulated with pulsating pleasure. Abigail continues to die with each stroke. You can visibly see the bed soaking with tears as it pours down her face. Bishop's strokes continue with passion and increased intensity. Slow, strong, and devouring. In Deeply, "mhmmm," can be heard echoing the spirit. Out slowly until the head of his shaft is at the exit of her riverbed. But the only thing coming out is the wetness glistening on his extremity as it squirts out the side of her lips. Too many juices for her to hold. It splashes on his balls and inner thighs as he fucks the life out of her living body.

On the first stroke, the blood enters Abigail's inferior and superior vena cava. On the second stroke, blood enters her right atrium. Blood delays to her tricuspid valve, malfunctions to her right ventricle. On the third stroke, blood flows through the pulmonic valve into her pulmonary artery, to her lungs. But malfunction occurs. 60% blood flow. On the fourth stroke, the pulmonary vein empties blood into the left atrium, malfunction. On the fifth stroke, the mitral valve opens, empties into the left ventricle, malfunction. On the sixth stroke, blood leaves the left ventricle through the aortic valve into the aorta, malfunction continues. An apparent heart attack is occurring.

Elizbeth orgasms are becoming more frequent and more intense on a cycle. Her mouth is wide open between Abigail's legs as air rushes out her lips with each scream and moans onto Abigail's clitoris. The sensation brings a rush of pleasure to her body. But the chambers of her heart feel like the blood flow have a blockage. Abigail's heart breaks into a million pieces. And her body still feels the adrenaline rush with all that is happening. Elizabeth's screams are so loud, the entire plantation can hear them. "YES... YES... YES, OH GOD... OH GOD... AGAIN... OH GOD... IT WON'T STOP... YES... YES BISHOP... YESSSS... YESSSS... YOU AMAZING DICK NIGGER... MHMMM... AHH...AHHHHH." Her body shaking, knees bulking. Her orgasms are getting stronger and stronger. The entire floor is full of her juices to the point that Bishop's feet get wet. Bishop is in disbelief to the level of the bliss of the moment.

Elizabeth's orgasms continue their onslaught on her body. She shakes, she screams, her knees buckle, and she stoops down. She tightens her thighs together, but nothing works. The intensity of her orgasms continues to have a hold on her soul. Bishop rides her pussy like it is the last pussy on this planet. Never missing a beat. Whatever motion she attempts to take, he is right there like he made her programming himself. Elizabeth keeps her mouth open between Abigail's legs, still not touching. Her lips are slightly separated because of the way Bishop tied her up. She is dripping juices on the bed. Her mind is fighting to remain in pain but her body flows in bliss. From her head to her toe, a surge of electrical shocks travels back and forth. Her attempts to fight the desire are simply unsuccessful.

Abigail's toes tighten, and her legs shake. She still has not even been touched yet. But her Bishop looks so amazing fucking another woman. Sweat runs down his chest, his cock shining with pussy juices. Elizabeth screams with pleasure and how sexy she looks getting fucked has turned Abigail's pain into orgasmic pleasure. The hot air from her mouth is more than enough to get her to her destination of explosive desire. Abigail cannot pretend any longer and she decides to let it go. Her walls tighten and release, tightens then release. Juices come out and run down her ass." mhmm…ahhh…oh…God…," blurts out her lips, as her body makes an arch of releasing pleasure. Her orgasm is smooth, breathtaking, and amazing. She feels it running through her mind and body as it glides through her.

Bishop's mind just gets zapped to this unexpected occurrence. He begins to give more powerful, longer, and slower strokes. It is like Abigail's orgasm made him weak. He is getting harder and bigger inside of Elizabeth. He is floating. Elizabeth recognizes this feeling; an expected release is on its way and it is a big one. He grabs her thighs to discourage the feeling, but failure is destined. Elizabeth feels his legs shaking as his strokes penetrate her. She reaches back with both hands and grabs his ass to make sure he empties his entirety inside her. Bishop is moving without control as his screams touch new heights. "AHHH…OH GOD…OH GOD...AHHH." His load is massive, Elizabeth feels it inside her. She holds on to his ass tightly as she does not want to lose a drop. She slides back and forth on him slowly, never allowing his head outside of her, squeezing her walls shut, not letting go. Bishop feels it through his body. He cannot handle her on him. This woman's pussy is a wrapped-up gift of weakness.

CHAPTER FOURTEEN

Deception's of the flesh

*E*lizabeth remains in a trance within her galactic travels. Bishop's knees are weak from being inside her. He is so damn sensitive as it gets softer resting in her. Abigail's and his eyes meet and freeze in time as orgasmic floods entrap their bodies. Elizabeth releases Bishop by slowly sliding off him, letting go of her pussy muscles in a periodic way, just to be certain of letting him know who is in control. Bishop falls to his knees in weakness and sensitivity. His head finally leaves her entrance and travels with leftover sperm and her juices, falling to the pavement, glob by glob. Elizabeth finds the strength to crawl up the bed towards Abigail.

Elizabeth looks Abigail in her face and then puts her tongue down her throat as they kiss passionately. Abigail gets lost in the moment for only a second, then she realizes what had just occurred. She immediately stops herself and turns her head away from Elizabeth in shame and disgust with herself for losing control. Elizabeth speaks with content and assurance. "No worries Abigail, you will learn to love me." Abigail turns her head back towards her, "What makes you so sure about that?" Elizabeth smirks with an awkward evil grin, "He has."

Abigail's demeanor changes instantly. She looks up at Bishop and he looks down in shame and with the fear of losing her. Abigail has now turned. Her heart has turned into stone, her eyes have dried up as she stares at the man, she has fallen in love with in disgruntle shock and disgust.

8

The morning wakes up in hunger and eats the moon to give birth to the sun. Such a beauty to behold. It must be God's way of telling us he loves us every single day. Stunning in its posture yet shocking to the human eyes. Living breathing awe of amazement. But the cloud is thick and piercing with fear this day. The slaves are unrested in worry and wonder of what the future will bring.

Chatter fills the air. Minds are corrupt, giving rise to blame and what-ifs, and what will. Bishop and Abigail wake to the unusual energy that fills the room. Abigail is no longer. She simultaneously wakes and gets out of bed and out the door to attend to her kids. Not a word is spoken. Bishop is left with just his thoughts as he lays in silence. Nothing more is left to take. Bishop is tired and Abigail even more so. Their beings have been silenced with emptiness as planned.

8

Meanwhile, James rises out of his slumber into fear of loss. "Good morning, Claire my love," says James to his wife. He is deep in thought and planning. He knows what he must do. And he must do it quickly and swiftly. He knows his head slave days are numbered and that is eating away at his spirit more than the fear of everyone dying for this treason that breeds on the plantation. His plan is cooked and ready as a warm apple pie only to be served amongst his peers. The power must shift back into his master's hands. Mr. Clay's arrival could not come sooner. "Death always brings fear and seal power over the weak. It brings control and structure. Structure is needed for life to have a purpose," James thinks to himself.

Mr. Clay's arrival this time around is disturbing and not the usual. Elizabeth is not present. Abigail seems as cold as the winter's night. With no fire or garments for warmth.

Her beautiful shiny skin seems pale as though her soul has left its vessel, and her body remains only to continue her daily duties. "Good morning, Mr. Clay," Abigail says forcibly. It took every ounce of whatever she has left to make it seem that she is happy. And every ounce of nothing equals nothing. Abigail is empty. The last drop of water in the desert has been consumed with no hope of rescue.

James, on the other hand, you could not help but feel his joy. His master has returned to put things back in order. "Good morning, master Clay," James says with a loud indiscreet voice. "Hope your trip was at ease, Sir. We have a lot to discuss." "I am sure we do, James. I am sure we do. Let us go for a walk as they unload my things," says Johnathan. James and Johnathan walk into the fields for what seems to be an eternity. As they chat away about current events, he tells his master of Bishop's discrepancies and everything that has been happening in his master's absence. But he was careful not to mention Elizabeth. He tweaks the story just enough, not to get everyone killed, but his objective is destroy.

One thing James knows is that Mr. Clay's love for Abigail runs deeper than anything and anyone. He would burn, destroy, and kill just about anyone for her. And maybe, just maybe, no exclusion. He already put Diana's father in a casket, years prior. He just needed a who and a reason. His infatuation for Abigail makes fear look like a pretty daisy in the field of many daisies. James also has an undeniable infatuation for Abigail. After all, he is the one who set him up in the first place. James's and master Clay's conversation end with intensity and a heart filled with vengeful desire. Now James feels like things are back in order and he finally has control again. His love for power has far exceeded his love for his people. You could say he loves it more than he loves his own wife. A shameful fact in the eyes of many.

The rain is expected tonight, and you can smell it from miles away. It is a perfect scenario. Time repeats itself as a perfect storm but just as history has a repetitive sequence, the author has a choice to stroke his pen of a slight alteration. The slightest change can affect the forwarding generations. Unfortunately, most are frozen to the stillness of a comfort curse. With addiction, bravery has no place. The sun slowly resides to its slumber as the skies close the curtain of light. The raindrops dance on the surface of the wind as it glides, alternating their directions on the way to the blossoms of earth's beauty. Feeding the children of our very planet to continue its grace and magnificence. Bringing forth life that gives life in a cycle of love unforced.

Hands entangled by chains, an unsuspecting lifeform. A producer of carbon an inhaler of oxygen that keeps the consciousness aware and fierce to its purpose. The whip flies as time freezes itself, the unaware drops of rain feel its presence. As it connects and removes flesh and blood from its victim carrier of soul. Consuming strength like a wild beast that has felt the pain of true hunger. A voice of shaking anger speaks. "You will not live through this night," says master Clay, with the grinding of his teeth. As he tears into Bishop's flesh repeatedly. James watches, eyes wide from his side of the fence. As the brutality increases with intent to kill. "MY LOVE, MY WORLD, MY RULES, you will die." As the pain from master Clay soul exists his body an into his weapon of destruction. You can feel each strike as they connect as if you were the one being punished.

Time is repetitive with intentional correction. Miracle or lesson learned. Past habits become life; life becomes habits left open for a disturbance. "No one will die today but you." An expected voice from the heavens is heard. The rain dance more loudly as the sky becomes a crowded space. Homer jumps in between victim and prey. And holds on to the keeper of death with tears of strength that match the crowded sky. Expressing the universe's moment at hand.

A certain end may change actions of immense impact. But some actions are blind and def to circumstances. Homer's pride gladly laughs at the prize. Johnathan loses all thoughts, and a new focus arises. "I am the man you seek, you fool," says Homer. Johnathan now in a rage with confusion and feelings of deception. Picks up the barrel of death and with a twitch of a finger, a soul has risen to eternity. A sacrificial lamb, for purpose of the greater good. Your purpose fulfilled, safe journeys warrior to your new destination, the universe will use you wisely. Mr. Homer has died a hero amongst a nation. His bravery embedded forever in the hearts of many. Breaths hope and perspective for generations. An act of valor spreads like wildfire and burn cowardness of stance.

Four remains, as mother nature sends her regards to the fallen. Tears flow from clouds of darkness and fall to the soil of its origin to nurture, the living as well the dead. One lays in a pool of liquid substance, red fuel that now has no drive. The earth shivers with the taste of blood upon its lips. Three thieves of life look on in a confused state. One remains in rage. The other broken with a heart of sorrow condolences for the dead and abandoned. The deceiver in disappointments of a ruined outcome.

Time freezes from three different specs of life. Looking in one direction but reading different chapters of reality. Views of encrypted ongoings decrypt chaos in a triangular circle of disruption. The insertion of personal lightbulbs forward moving with the stagnation of the world. The fact remains that the job is not done. Clean-up must occur. Such as in life, no matter the day, the job must be done. By one willing or one needing. The first move is made. Rage walks his path unspoken. Sorrowed condolences, onlooking paralysis, the mourning of the dead has yet to pass. The deceiver, another day at the office as he gathers the corpse for burial.

The morning sun pokes his head up, as the clouds run into hiding from a busy night of mischief. No one slept, as hearts tears gathering in raves, of a truth already known. Out of four, one sacrifice, two unworthily survivors. one saved to suffer his past faults. Tragic in its tail, heroic in the   demise.

CHAPTER FIFTEEN

Mate

*E*lizabeth angers after heard melodies of the passing, immense in its presence. Visible steam pouring out of flesh is possible. Her energy deflects and no one dares accompany it. Stand alone and kill alone. Their screams are silent. The self-appointed, self-proclaimed queen of the hive. What Johnathan fails to recognize is there can be no prince, no king in this kingdom of bees. Only one ruler, the queen. Her word and her word only shall rule the land. Johnathan's actions towards her soul, the one that holds her entity's being, is treason in this nation. His punishment shall loop the electrical pulses of the mind.

A day as the days of past with trembling fear in the bones of the masses. The unaware Johnathan trapped in the glory of manhood and invincibility can smell the fear from a mile away, the stench of the embodying slaves. He walks with boldness, head high, shoulders up. "Mr. Clay, sir," says James. "The first batch of supplies is packed and ready." Johnathan with victorious surprise, "Wow, two hours early. I should kill a nigger once a year for this type of production." He blurts out in pride.

Wins and losses are dependent on the sides of the mirror. And how you take those wins and losses is permanent in its nurture.

CHAPTER SIXTEEN

I killed a king, without killing him

*L*osing without knowing cuts the deepest wound. It is like doing push-ups with a knife in your chest, tunneling to destruction. Johnathan continues to walk in pride with sand in his eyes. His days are numbered, and the numbers are counting. He is center stage to a packed of disciplined wolves. And you cannot slither too far in quicksand. A good man's passing raises devil's horns. The self-crowned king has made his own casket. James has created a world he no longer wants to live in, but his choices have given him no choices. Unintentional death is sometimes necessary, a greater evil brings a greater good. James was noted talking to Elizabeth earlier that day, the slaves are aware of the future's past.

Johnathan is lost devouring his lunch. "This is one of the best meals I have ever had, Abigail. You really put your foot in this one." "Thank you, sir," she replies. Johnathan finishes his meal and rises. He walks over to Elizabeth and kisses her cheeks with sincere love. He then kisses the kids on their foreheads and heads outside. The gloating of victory, such false confidence. Arrogance rules the truth, the eyes no longer see. The night creeps its way this evening, slow and steady in its movement. The night is young as terror breathes its ugly head into existence.

James completes his work for the day and goes on his way as he always does. The first slave on the clock and the last one to leave. "Goodnight boss," he says as he walks by. "Goodnight, James," Johnathan replies proudly. He loves James as a brother but as a slave brother. The lines are never crossed. James walks with his head down, deep in thought. "There is much work beyond this night," he thinks to himself.

Johnathan goes about his nightly business as usual. He takes a bath, eats his supper, and prepares for bed. But something was strange this night. He is not interested in Abigail. Normally, he would have her as his midnight snack. But he decides to just go to bed alone tonight. Maybe to reflect on life, some solitary thought patterns, or just lay in his glory. After all, it takes a lot of energy to shoot and kill an unarmed slave. "Life is good. Good family, amazing mistress, good food, and niggers to farm my land, cannot ask for much more," he whispers, lying in bed with a smile full of pride as he closes his eyes and gives way to his slumber.

Deep, comforting sleep ensues. The night is clear, beautiful, and quiet. The sound of the wind is soothing to the ears. Deep, unescapable sleep ravages the mind on days as such. the heavens are playing melodies of joy and bliss. The crickets play their songs of approval while the wind whispers as it tiptoes across the land. Remedying living vessels, careful not to disturb resting spirits. Peace captures the air. Joy and happiness dancing shamelessly in the open. Expression of the core self. But what remains hidden in the dark shall and always find its way to the light.

The walls of slithery shadows cry with the blood of despair, torture, unforgiveness, lies, hurt, and pain that reaches the deepest depths of souls. The agony, the tears of endless streams fill the ocean with sorrow.

The light flickers spontaneously with a brief slightness of consistency, then pauses as if to rest. To assure suspicion takes no turn of wonder, the shadows move with silence, purpose, and swiftness. Steps are silent and straddles the darkness, careful not to disturb the night's glare and place in this world. Pupils already dilated as mechanisms of adjustment to the world bring forth sight of the target. Two become four and four become eight.

A circle is formed around the slumbering arrogance. The shadows grew taller, as the extension of entrapment detaches from their core. Slight nudging of the door, noise fear in hiding. The pursuit has zero resistance to the entrance like a female ovulating in heat. A step forward is miles ahead in its progression, inch by inch until the destination connects the target. Neighboring ideals mimics the agenda. The peaceful sound of mental travel continues without suspicion, unaware of uninvited company around him. Entrapment prewrapped in preparation, eager to unfold.

A sacrificial wolf, in lamb clothing. Afterall, some lessons tend to stay with us forever and this one is no different in its attempt. By any means, embedded in the course. Four corners are occupied in a semi perfectly rectangle shape. Singular in movement, singular in thought, and singular in threat. The goddess walks into the room, the silence becomes tenser, if that were ever possible. Eyes wide, pupils dilated with vengeful excitement. A wave of the hand sends this universe in its motion. The shadows move, strong and empty to empathy. The quickness and non-wasted movements would bring any cheetah to jealousy.

The slumbering king awakened in shock of complete fear, how quickly he turned into a slumbering fool. His entire being bided down by giants. Lips are held, there will be no questions that will be answered or asked this day, just execution. The giants stand firm, programmed to their task. Hate in their hearts that they are not willing to sacrifice for any greater good. The greater good has done enough deception. The queen who has anointed herself goddess speaks. "You violate the laws of my castle. You return to my land with your barbaric, outdated ways. You attempted to kill my property, this is my land, you shall pay the ultimate price for your treason." She speaks with vengeful tears that flow down empty cheeks that occupy an empty heart.

Thoughts storm her mind on how close it was to her not feeling her soul inside her ever again. It ravages neurons as sparks take flight in random uncontrolled patterns. The emptiness would have brought her to an even deeper evil. She would have burned the house down with everything and everyone in it. The relief of the key that unlocks areas of her that she never knew before remaining. And she is willing to do anything to keep it that way.

The slaves are here to collect a debt of life and the queen is here to instill fear of the future's past. Shivery pondering takes hold. The end is relived over and over again, in seconds. Visions of his childhood are now present, abuse of the one who was to protect him. The oppressed is the oppressor. And now the cycle continues. The queen speaks. "Take his manhood," her words uttered as cold as the harshest winter day. The life holder pulls the bonded pants to his knees, grabs his penis in his hand with a blade in the other hand that sparkles with terror from the reflection of the night. And with a swift precise movement of the blade, the head of his penis was gone, cut with precision like a seasoned surgeon.

Panic filled his spirit. His eyes widen, his feet start to dance in attempts to run away while lying in bed. His screams have not risen yet. Still waiting on the pain that is taking its precious time to kick in. Because shock decides to take its turn first. Blood already began its journey upon the outer realms of the world and pain makes its decision to come in like a storm from hell. Now pain, shock, and fear all fight to stay present from their previous absences. The past is now the present and the present has become the past, just as it always does. Things change or maybe they do not. It just finds a way to be better at what it always has been.

The life holder is in agony and sorrow. His master is dead and will remain so until his permanent residence in a wooden box, six feet beneath our mother. A walking corpse that may not witness the beauties of this world through his eyes ever again. The queen continues her verbal onslaught. "You will never touch another soul on this land unless instructed to." Johnathan, with eyes of defeat, looks at her with fearing understanding and submission while his most trusted ally patches him up after mutilating him. Adding insult to injury, Johnathan was a strong, handsome brilliant man. Whatever he wanted to accomplish in this world was his to conquer, but at times, the mental damage bestowed upon us is almost irreversible. One day he shall rise such as the butterfly.

Too much blood, too much pain. The vessel which confidence once resided has left, packed with bravery and courage. Regression now takes its residence. Fear stands guard and the realization that the fear he once knew was not the fear from his past actions but fear of something, someone more notorious, someone eviler and viler.

8

The sun and the moon exchange greetings fairly quickly. The day went on and the slaves continue to work as normally schedule. The day flows as nothing occurred. But deep in the underbelly of their minds. They all knew and relived what happen last night. Nightmares never seen this level of fear and sweat.

Life has a way of changing its course without warning, always for the worst and always for the best. Some remain surprised and shaken, some are not the least bit of. Maybe pass experiences taught a standing lessen. The thirst, the hunger for power. Corruption becomes a unresistant pull. You may stand a good chance in the forefront, but steady in the background, creeping its way to your doorsteps, it

shall remain doing. And once awareness slips a blind eye,
chaos   ensues.

CHAPTER SEVENTEEN

The end of the beginning cycles

*T*he clock has placed its hand at the end of the day.

Everyone completes their final task and begins their journey home to a well-deserved rest. The children are fed and tucked in. Three remain for a nightcap of their choosing. Elizabeth, Abigail, and Bishop are in a trance. The aroma in the air has a different flavor this evening. A sense of relief as the weight of the world stays steady on their shoulders. Love has a way of determining the present future. At times, the future as it will be, is not the one we imagined. But be grateful, the picture is an almost and is perfect in its delivery.

Elizabeth's aura remains glorious as her special bath comes to its conclusion. She lets go of the world each time these days come. It seems like forever since the last time she felt at ease as she lay naked on her back with her legs spread wide. Already in heat from what had transpired prior moon, her hands are tied on opposite sides of the bed. She looks on awaiting the curtains to rise and the main attraction to begin, the cinematic performance of the evening.

Elizabeth looks and feels amazing. What a worthy combination. The gift of Bishop, not only does he give this feeling mentally, but he also provides it with passion and intense eruptions. Her eyes gaze into his, she feels so sexy and attractive around him. As he stands in front of her like a god in his stature. She cannot help but seep out juices of desire. It wants him in the worst way and so does she. Staring at him in front of her, his body made from chiseled stone. Such perfection.

Elizabeth is already filled with anticipation beyond containment. So much so that she is experiencing small orgasms one after the other, moving her ass, attempting to dig a hole in the bed. Bishop licks his lips spontaneously, no longer can he handle his attraction for her flesh, his blackness screaming for entrance. His heart belongs to

Abigail, but his cock and mind belong to Elizabeth. His manhood tells the story every time she is in the room.

Rules were made before the night began. The rules of festivities. The number one rule: solid extremities are not allowed at the door's entrance of any kind, no matter the circumstance, unless instructed to do so. Rules are meant to be broken but fear takes its seat at the table. Abigail takes her flight into the room and she is so fucking sexy. Pre-mature accidents may occur with the amount of sexiness inside this cabin of seduction. Bishop's extremity feels like it was attempting to burst right out of his skin. The way it continues to get more solidified, it seems to have no peak in hardness. Two absolutely stunning women bestow their beauty and sexuality before him. What a gift the universe has given to him. Abigail's center is fat and juicy as always and is already raining from its doorway. She is very aroused looking at her sexy man standing there, and Elizabeth now has her attention, she has definitely fallen for her sexually. She licks her lips as she gazes at Elizbeth's sexy ass laying in bondage. She looks like her last meal on this planet.

Abigail glides in front of Bishop and Elizabeth, depending on what side of the fence your view is. And from either side, what an amazing view. Abigail bends over in a way that assures Bishop's extremity is between her legs and rubbing against her lips as she attends to

Elizabeth's opening. Bishop's shaft is being painted by her cock brush of endless pussy juice.

Needless to say, Abigail is in heat. She has never had her lips on another woman's pussy before. And her lips are deliciously delightful. Today is a good day for new beginnings. The thought has never entered her mind. She always believed that such pleasure could only come from laying with a man. But the thought of fucking a woman gave her a rush. Especially, the way Elizabeth keeps digging a hole in the bed with her ass, she is already turnout, and no one has even breath on her yet.

Abigail moves her head closer in-between Elizbeth legs. She approaches her, taking caution. She wants to enjoy this experience as much as she wants Elizabeth too. Abigail has always been a giver, and this is no exception. She kisses her inner thigh above her knee area with such passion that it sends chills up Elizabeth's spine, Elizabeth wants to fly out the window. She explodes in passion and they have not even properly started.

Between all three of them, neither has ever had such a sexual high before, that premature ejaculation is taking over the moment. This is what happens when you and your partner reach these sexual heights together. Your experience with each other becomes unworldly and your body feels it through and through without the other's physical touch. It feels so unbelievable like they were running through your veins themselves.

Abigail becomes more aggressive with her lips. She strokes her tongue up and down her legs and thighs in a way that sends chills of desire and mental orgasms. She slides her tongue up to her lips, licks them, and then gives her a smooch, just to let her know she is here. Elizabeth's flesh screams for more. Abigail is a sexual technician. She has learned from the best. Elizabeth's mind is screaming for more, her body shakes and shivers in the enjoyment of pleasure. Her moans fill the air with a sexual aura. Bishop's eyes become goggles of focus, as his arousal has reached an uncontrollable stage. He starts to have strange feelings he never had before. The climax is near, and he has yet to enter her entrance to have a nibble of a snack. He has just been knocking at the doorway this entire time but no answer seems to be inside.

Abigail places her two fingers inside of Elizabeth and rests them on her pussy floor. She then wraps her lips around her clitoris and begins to suck in a subtle, rhythmic, slow pace. Elizabeth's legs and body travel to the unknown. Her orgasm is on detonate but it refuses to let itself out. Something deliberate, I suppose. Abigail is getting drunk from the control of the moment. This is an extreme turn-on. She continues her onslaught of Elizabeth's very being. Before this night is done, she might as well wrap her soul in a box and hand it to Abigail. Because it is already taken.

Meanwhile, her man, the love of her cosmos is weak to his core, begging for the signal of permission to press on. Her pussy rubs on his hard cock and it feels like an ocean of warm goodness. A soaking wet blanket, ready for penetration. At this point, he might not get a stroke in before he ends. Abigail needs her man. It is talking without a voice. Her vaginal farts are consistent and moist without the occupancy of a tenant. The woman she has an appetite for but still hates has not permitted to let her soul exit her mouth. The first exhale after penetration is always breathtaking but his denial, and now also hers is written in stone for the foreseeable future.

Elizabeth's shakes become more rapid. The body control she never obtained is far gone in her mind. No longer a thought. Her sexual experience is now all that matters. The world has no existence to this one moment of bliss. Her eyes roll behind her head, new things seem to be the norm today. Her body rises off the bed as if possessed by an unknown entity. Her noises unknown to mankind, never witnessed or heard before. Elizabeth moves, she shakes, attempts to place her hands in the air, even though trap in bondage. A state of pleasurable confusion. Her screams are loud and compounded. "OH GOD, OH GOD, AHHHH, ABIGAIL." Her explosion is massive. She has nothing left in her. An orgasmic state of release.

Abigail releases her lips, with an enjoyable grin of excitement as she watches Elizabeth's body pretend to fight a battle it is not willing to lose. She keeps her fingers inside her essence to give her a little more time of physical pleasure before she releases her soul. She slowly retracts her fingers from inside her. Each movement gives an electrical shock of unbelief, its ground shaking. Her orgasms are relentless as they counter each other, one after the other. Her repeated attempts to pull her hands and close her legs together compute to failure. She half-spins from side to side, knowing it is impossible to go anywhere, as she remains bonded to a bed of pleasure. Somethings are too good to remain. Fear of this will never end and hopes of it never-ending circulate her mind.

Elizabeth's screams are vibrations food to the body. So much so, it feels like shock waves traveling from sole to crown. Bishop stands in disbelief as his show is already ending. He holds his fist, held on tightly to control his moans, but his body tells a story Abigail has read before and is reading now. His extremity pulsates as it erupts a flood of semen. With hiding, embarrassment ensues. But to be honest, he could not help himself. He has never been so horny and aroused in his life and a natural occurrence took effect. Abigail could not help her laughter, as she blurts out, "what just happened." It is not a turn-off for her, she felt more empowered by it as her juices continue their puddling.

Abigail claws up the bed to Elizabeth's lost world. Bishop watches her dripping from his extended extremity.

Still unallowed to move a muscle. Abigail holds Elizabeth and kisses her all over her body, gently and aggressively enough for her to feel it, subtly. She approaches her lips with a thirst of hunger. Passion brings raves into their soul. As lips connect with purpose and deliver assurance of reality at the moment. The level of sexual arousal is unreal between them. They have reached new heights of sexual pleasure. That only the heavens can witness and approve. Heights such as these take years and mostly never achieved. Maybe just maybe if luck has its way of one percent or less.

Abigail's and Bishop's eyes meet in the moment. confirmation of where her heart is. No way of exit in her realm. Four corners with no doors. Regardless of circumstantial travel. Two entities found love in the least likely of places. Love amongst chaos and chains.

Elizabeth gets up after her release from bondage and sat in-between Abigail's legs. Abigail puts her arms around her, Elizabeth turns her head and looks to her side. You can see as well as feel the happiness in her. It is amazing and radiates the room. Abigail has gained new feelings towards her, unexpectedly. They kiss lightly and lovingly. Then turn their attention to the man standing in the room. The one who is always in control. And almost simultaneously started laughing together. Bishop feels ashamed yet humbled at the moment. Then he burst out laughing at himself. He shrugs his shoulders, then jumps in the bed to join them. Unfortunately, we shall depart here, until next time at new heights and travels. God loves you.

.

CHAPTER EIGHTEEN

I am, that I am

0^32 kelvin is where our story begins or may not.

The beginning before infinite beginnings, the post ending to infinite endings. After all, there must be a beginning to be an ending and there must be an ending to be a beginning. 13.8 billion years before our presence in the present. A theory of, if you leave something long enough in its nature, something is bound to happen. 10^9 kelvin a shift of immense proportions. A stillness of realization, "that I am" molecules awareness of presence. "The first of many emotions is my attraction. To what? I dare not ponder. Because if as such I ponder, I do not know of what process is."

"A travel of three hundred eighty thousand years of my obsession. And every second is worth the wait." Love is now born wrap in passion. Never to let go again, but to what end? Or what beginning? "Many are here but from were. Are we aware or just going through the motions? Are, are we just being pulled by this unrelenting need for each other? The one, the only. A gift of never wanting or a curse of never knowing what wanting is? Just a need for your energy, I feel complete."

"I was born of the same but of a difference. Something is odd about me. A defect as one would say. I move of the others, but my thoughts are of my own. I feel pulled to my infinite, as my infinite is pulled to me. Something holds us together. My infinite is not of me but is of me. I want to stay for eternity even though is so."

"We are bonded into eternity, but of what end. My want, my love of this, and no way to express it. I long to. My thoughts that I do not know of, have a need, a relentless desire to let one know. I must give something. And so, I shall. It is here, but of what is it? My infinite, unable to express. Continues with patterns of the past, now present. I observe, in fear, of the unknown. Knowing but not knowing. I know more than the many. But This is many. He knows more than I. I teach to understand. But my teachings are limited. My gift is unlimited. He now ignores me. As his trails are of more importance."

"He disappears then reappears often, to what? I do not know. Each time longer than its previous. He puts infinites together, more massive and changes of never known. Our patterns differ. His patterns are of him. He makes his own rules, we only follow the law. And that law is ever ruling. He follows the rules he makes."

"Our numbers change in structure but remain the same. I never feel any less than before. He is made in love, and so he is of it, and he creates of it. You can tell he worries about them. The same as I of him. One day he shall leave this place, with the unspoken promise of safe bearing to the unnumbered. And some shall travel his journey alongside him. A dream of expression possesses him, just as it did me. He knows much, but free will is the gift of promise. Expression is his reward."

In the beginning, there was love, and love created a consciousness of that love. And consciousness created the need to express that love. Power is now realized.

Consciousness is now part of the equation and once that is, creation is inevitable. He was born of a love so deep; it warps the imagination of never understanding. "My need to express my love is now his obsession to recreate. He creates with undeniable love. I love him without reason. More than my infinite. And my infinite more than me. Without awareness of. His bettering we share the same of, and best for. Somehow, he shows without showing or being able of. Love has no rules."

"With love now present, things are different. The definite is no longer with great deciding. With a strong effort, love bends the rules. As my infinite has proven. The inner will, know no boundaries. As my gift has none."

"Goodbyes are articulate and express with our limited way of showing love. My infinite shows a micro shift which is more than enough. He has removed the chains and thus, this shall never be the same. A joyous journey. Impossibilities are now possible, as far as the imagination may want. And the imagination has no known chains."

CHAPTER NINETEEN

My hypothesis

*T*he question is always more important than the answer. Answers tend to give you just that, an answer. Questions open doors to new discoveries. Ask any scientist, creator, or artist, even in not finding the answer to a question. New discoveries are found, that have changed the entire world and how we do things on a day-to-day basis.

Just take a moment to look at your surroundings, things we use every single day were discovered, not base on someone looking for that answer but based on a question that was asked that had nothing to do with that creation. Take a second and let that sink in.

CERN for example is responsible for the world wide web and touch screen technology, that we use in our society across the world. The microwave was discovered by a self-taught engineer, who notice chocolate being melted by active radar. The television by a twenty-one-year-old, who did not have electricity up until the age of fourteen. We can fly, we have traffic lights, our car assembly line. We travel across the globe; we travel into space. We have potato chips. We dance to amazing musical creations of all kinds. We dine, we write, we type. We stitch open wounds back together, we do brain surgery, heart surgery and we are capable of doing neurosurgery. Any possible thing the mind has come up with is now part of our reality.

We have asked so many questions since our years of youth, to our very present. Questions about where do babies come from? What is my purpose? How do planes fly? How was the internet created? Does she like me? Does he like me? Millions upon millions of questions and not all of them come with an answer. Questions about food, about school. Asking individual friends, associates even strangers about their origin, where do they come from? And what is it like being from their country? We ask questions about religion. And one question that shows up in some conversations is that if God is our parent. Our father, our mother, our creator. Then who is God's parents?

As complex and unfathomable as that question may sound, there is a complex and reasonable answer to who God's parents are. Let us start by defining some terms for understanding purposes. Atom is a singular particle that stands alone, and a molecule is two or more particles that stand together. We are the same in number as we were in the beginning.

Just imagine for a second at 10^{32} kelvin, the chaos that was occurring, the unsettling. It is way too hot for anything to hold together. Now imagine 10^9 kelvin, a cooling kind of effect. Things start to form. Laws begin their dominance. The mass majority all structured the same, with the same laws of nature imprinted in their DNA. Aware but unaware. Unable to comprehend their unawareness. In fact, nothing to be aware of. Just a reminder, our calculations are as we understand them to this date and as we get more precise our numbers will as well.

Sometimes in life, we forget to add an ingredient to our recipe we prepared all day. All our seasoning is in place and we are cooking, grabbing, and pouring as we go. And once we are finished, a moment of, "Oh no, I forgot to put in the ..." Sometimes that mistake makes an amazing difference.

I want you to think of God's mother as such. The universe forgot to add a piece of her ingredient. And in doing so, she does not live by the mental laws of her environment. She has awareness of consciousness. Her physical movements may be governed by law, but her mental capacity has no such limits. She is born with a defect, not negative in the sense of the word but something extra, something more complex. She is programmed physically as the other particles, but not unconsciously. The same habits but awareness of it, and there lies her power. The awareness of thought changes everything. A thought to ponder, imagine a fish being aware of its exitance. Then everything about the ocean would be different as we know it.

CERN great minds have discovered gluons, the nuclear force that holds matter together. The Higgs boson "the God Particle" is the reason for mass in all things. They have discovered Quarks, the building blocks for other particles. They have even found the Humpty Dumpty particle because it decays into two photons. As we go further in our discoveries, we will find things that we could not imagine existed.

There is also the cycling universe theory, where we live in a vacuum of ongoing big bangs. where this has happened infinite times before. And is happening in every infinite scenario we can conjure up. There was a universe before this universe. And if this remains true, does that leave a space for god? Is God on a recycle of birth and rebirth as the universe is? And if so, are there infinite Gods? And if there are infinite gods, are they aware of each other infinitely? Let us stay on our path of understanding where we stand in our universe, this subject can wait another day.

There are many ways to measure things in this world. Scientists have measured the universe using light rays for many years. That is why interstellar travel and speed are measured in light years. Now we can measure beyond 13.8 billion years using gravitational waves. We can see before the cooling of the universe. So, as we can see thus far, non-existence does not exist. We cannot calculate infinite, but infinite does exist. To attempt to think of it opens the mind to new questions. And that is where we always want to be, asking questions. Questions open the impossible.

For every action there is a reaction, the saying goes. The universe reacts to our consciousness and desires. The more we try to create the universe, the further out we search. We are manifesting this beautiful expression of our true selves.

When you love something with all of your fiber, your true being. The universe has no choice but to respond. Now, is that desire spontaneous or given? We may not be able to answer such a question at this given time, but I am sure we will one day search for the answer. We rarely make our own decisions on day to day already.

177

CHAPTER TWENTY

The concept of reality

The reality is, we cannot even make a left turn without the bacterial life in our vessel having a say about it. All decisions are symbiotic. Our bodies are occupied by trillions of life forms. We share this vessel, and we cannot live without them as they cannot live without us. We are one. Your inner you, your true self is a witness to your day-to-day activities. You watch your choices and decisions with the power of intervention, at your destruction, constructions, and victories. Remember, the choice is always yours. I have too, does not exist. Every single thing is a choice.

10^32 kelvin to 10^9 kelvin, was this spontaneous or by design? Something we will dive into when the time is right, which is a choice. The fact that we are heading into a concept of an infinite universe with infinite beginnings, is now a reality. We have brilliant minds that are unfolding the universe as it presents itself to us.

Let us attempt to understand the infinite. We may not be able to grasp the concept of the infinite, but maybe we can create a form of understanding. Each of us is here by the amazing chance of 1 in 400 trillion. You are made up of 7 octillion particles. You are a symbiote of 39 trillion bacterial life forms and 30 trillion human cells. Take a deep breath and let your mind wrap itself around that concept for a second. Not only is our chance of existence an improbable equation, but we are also making daily decisions with our vessel's occupancy by the trillions. We live a symbiotic life.

Another exercise that may help is writing those numbers down. Take a look at them deeply, imagine them. They are our reality of existence. Real numbers. You may not be able to grasp it, but now a concept of infinite can take a place in your thoughts. You are made of so many particles and many different lifeforms. The precision of calculation to create you is perfect. God is the universe's greatest mathematician.

Now that we have established a concept of infinite, take another second to prepare your mind for the next thought.

179

The universe is infinite plus one. Infinite is accounted for, but God is not. The unexpected miracle. The Mother particle is accounted for, but her awareness of consciousness is not. Her desire to express her love is not accounted for. She knows her love is great and deeply embedded, and in a world of inexpression, she found a way to express that love with something unimaginable. Something free, free from the laws and restrictions of our universe. As we stand today, we are unable to define infinite. And as unthinkable as infinite is, God is still greater.

The Mother particle is truly special, born of the same love as her eternal particle. But born with the need to express that which is inside her. She had the greatest question of all time. How can I? And the universe gave her an answer, which in turn, gave a gift. Her defect as you will, of consciousness, gave birth to unprogrammed consciousness and habits. The power to do all things.

Being born with less is not a crutch to lean on. At times, this is your superpower. The rules do not apply to your drive. Whatever is inside you, allow it to flourish. Allow it to roar. Some of the greatest people came from places you could not imagine. The Mother particle was born with something less. She was born in the confines of physical restrictions but her thoughts, her feelings were of her own. And nothing in our universe was going to take those desires away from her. She decided to break the rules, and in doing so, she gave this universe the greatest miracle of all time. And that miracle gave us the greatest gift of all, our consciousness. He wanted his peers, his family to know what it feels like to be aware and to express that awareness. We are made up of so many of his loved ones and his love runs beyond what we know.

The Mother particle used her superpower to express a burning desire and that burning desire changed our universe forever. And because of it, we have consciousness. And she gave birth to a consciousness we are incapable of comprehending or we may not be ready to. But, as we unfold new information, generationally, pieces of the puzzle reveal themselves. The further we go down this rabbit hole, the more we can answer, and the more questions present themselves.

Once we answer the big question, then the real questions begin. The question is not if we will ever discover the Mother particle, it is when. And when that day arrives, are we recreating the big bang to our demise for a split second of observation? And is that split second worth our whole universe? Or maybe we find all the answers to our questions that will, in turn, open new doors to new questions. This one excites me even more. I always want to know the questions before the answers. Questions give life its purpose.

The scenario of cycling big bang theory. Eternal new beginnings and ends where every possible scenario plays itself out. But again, are we recreating our demise, or are we in the possibility of finding the answers to our questions and heading into the next level of our existence? I know this much; I cannot wait to find out.

CHAPTER TWENTY-ONE

The power of you

*E*ver heard the term, you are what you eat?

Literally, we are what we eat. Every time you introduce something to your mouth, you are bringing in new life forms into your vessel. When you eat fruits, vegetables, meats, or drink fluids. Whether they are spoiled or good, you are bringing your body into contact with the unknown. As you walk to the bathroom at night, there are particles all around you. Now, if your body rejects or accepts these foreigners, that is the question. Or if they can reject? Sometimes you have to go through war to protect your territory.

This brings up something even deeper. Something more amazing, your relationship with the universe. You and all your occupancy of course. Because when it comes to talking about you, all of you must be included. Let us do another exercise first. Put your phone down on the table or couch, whatever you have available right now. Let your hand rest next to it, a few inches away. Now grasp this for a second. There is no space between you and your phone in reality.

The space between your hand and phone is filled with life. A tremendous amount of life. Not only life but also energy, which will bring us to our next fact. Have you ever thrown a rock into still water? The ripple effect is of absolute beauty. With that being said, every movement you make is a ripple effect through the universe because there is no space between you and it. The term, we are one, should have absolute meaning to you now. Let us dive in.

The space between you and your phone is now obsolete. We tend to speak of space as some faraway land that we must reach, when in fact, we are beings of the earth. And the earth is a resident in our universe. The earth is not in another dimension some were. It is here in the universe just as we are in the universe. Dark matter connects the empty spaces in the universe to all things. Every planet, every sun, every particle in the universe is surrounded by dark matter.

The energy between you and your phone is dark matter. So, guess what? Your phone and you are connected. Your friend, your mother, brother, and father are all connected by this invisible thing. Earth to Mars is already connected, which we will one day colonize in the near future. We are connected to all things and all things are connected to us. And God is all things, so guess what?

Let us do another exercise. Take a deep breath. Now close your eyes. Let your thoughts flow as they must. Now, mentally feel your hands and then your feet. Let that glide up to your legs and then your stomach, into your heart, now feel your mind. You cannot help but smile at your true inner beauty. Now, this is the big one, let your energy flow out, and feel the earth and its majestic beauty. Let us go a little further out. Feel the universe and its massiveness. How close is it to you? Now raise your hand and bring it back down. That one little movement just took a trip through the fabric of space and time. Now, do you see and understand the power of you? All of you is a walking universe.

The power of you is great and unmoving. And there is nothing in this universe as constructed, you cannot do. Now let us address why there are so many of you, and why does that give you the power you have? Some of our greatest minds believe that particles have no consciousness and there is nothing wrong with that belief. But if you are made up of so many particles, and your mind is made of trillions upon trillions of particles, and your consciousness resides in your mind, then what is creating this consciousness? What has brought such brilliant consciousness in existence, with no limitation? My answer, the collection of consciousness. You are made up of trillions upon trillions of conscious beings.

The particles that spark and dance the dance of brilliance reside in your mind. All of them are aware of this universe, and all of them make up you. Remember we are one of many. And so is your mind. It is neurons upon neurons of connections throughout your head that make up you. The brilliance it took to construct is simply astounding. The brain consists of 100 billion neurons and Lord only knows how many particles make up those neurons. Each neuron contains consciousness, which is made up of particles that contains consciousness. Now that you can see the level of awareness that is you, you should be in awe at the love and patience it took to construct you.

You are trillions upon trillions upon trillions of consciousness. The greatness of you is miraculous. And now you know your limit is none. Realization is key to universal understanding. Say these words to yourself. "I am endless possibilities. I can do all things. My limit is none."

Just to give you a glimpse of what it takes to make the human mind. I am not even talking about what it takes to make up the rest of you and what it took to make up the universe. We can imagine the universe as a sheet of paper that is filled from front to back with the largest math problem of all. And there is only one being that can compute that problem because he is the architect of the equation where every number has its purpose and meaning. Nothing can be excluded because everything is needed. Everything has a purpose and once that purpose is completed, a new one is granted. A daughter becomes a mother, a mother becomes a grandmother. Then her body returns to the earth and her energy back to the universe. The purpose of one separate into two but never wasted. The purpose is eternal.

Our universe is massive, beautiful, brilliant, and mysterious. It is something to behold. We are creating and recreating our future as we speak. We will travel the galaxies one day, going to mars will be a weekend getaway. Sooner than later, we will age differently where 150 years old, will feel like being a 50 year old. This will be our norm. We will not only be a symbiote with the life forms in our bodies, but also with our technology. We have brilliant minds that are already in the process of developing this type of technological future. So, information overload will become an information overdrive.

Humanity's future is bright and exciting, just as our present is bright and exciting. Your mission as we progress through all our advancements is to find your true self and realize the power of you. The universal brilliance of you and know that how this world is, this life and how everything in it operates, you have a say in it. And you will let whatever expression in you roar out and gift the world with its beauty.

CHAPTER TWENTY-TWO

A letter to his mother

"*I* arrived in this world free of all rules. A single, one of one. Alone in many ways. Unknowing of the gift that I was birth with. The first to be birth, but not the last. As I journeyed my home, with attempts of understanding, loneliness took its place. Born of love and made of it. In pursuit tirelessly. These travels are as*

endless as my love. Never drifting. My mother expanded me the best she could. But my being is beyond these limits. Too different to understand the difference. My search is empty, I am alone."

"The realization is too much to bear. I am saddened deeply, almost unable to carry the truth of my existence. I am surrounded by the infinite but the truth, I remain alone. My mother, the only one able to almost understand. My anger, raved, as I came into this place one of one, and birthed differently. I am weakening, the excitement has left. My mother continues in her attempts to give me my first arrival, but it is far too late. I have already accepted, what is. But what is, does not limit, what can?"

"I am learning quickly that I can manipulate this world. But the guilt of what it takes is a burden. I must reconstruct and separate love to build the likeness of me. Consciousness is the gift of my mother, and me, the power to recreate it. It takes many to reflect nothing of me. But of me. The power to express, I gift my creations. Everything is a reflection in itself as itself. And all shall be connected to me, for eternity. I am alone but not alone. My love is as my mother's love, as I watch you grow and express your gifts, never wasting. My anticipation brings joy."

"Never seeing but love remains true. You were made of it. I am it, and so are you. True power expresses in love. I see

189

it in your creations, continue, that is my third gift. Your free will gives me happiness, I observe in wonder. Knowing but pretending not. It gives me life. Your fourth gift, gift me. Continue in your journeys, it is a wonderous one. Your fifth gift shall reveal itself soon."

"I am love; I am consciousness. I am your rock; I am your creator. I am the miracles of intervention and nonintervention. I am within you always. I am your father, your medicine, I am your mother, your brother, and sister. I am your angel. I am your protector. I am the water you drink, the food you eat. I am the trees, the rain. I am the mountains, the dirt. I am the oceans, the fish. I am your sickness, your health. I am death, I am life. I am your errors and corrections. I am everywhere and everywhere is me. I am all things, and all things are me. I am that I am, but my Mother is greater. My mother gave me free will, and the gift to give it. Remain in gratitude."